HIDE AND SEEK
FOR LOVE

She had not got into her bed and although she was undressed she had taken some time in arranging her riding habit on a chair so that it would be ready for her when she awoke in the morning.

Benina knew that she must not keep David waiting as her father always said there was nothing more annoying than unpunctual women, believing it a man's duty to wait for them.

She put her riding boots in front of the chair.

Then she walked over to the window to have a last look at the moonlight.

The garden was a Fairyland and as she gazed down at the lake she thought what fun it had been to swim with David.

'I am so lucky,' she thought. 'If it had been anyone else he might have been as unkind and cruel as the Marquis and sent Nanny and me away from Ingle Hall.'

And how thrilled the pensioners would be at all he had done for them.

She was sure no other man would be so generous when he had so little money.

'He is wonderful! Wonderful!' she told herself.

THE BARBARA CARTLAND PINK COLLECTION

Titles in this series

HIDE AND SEEK
FOR LOVE

BARBARA CARTLAND

Barbaracartland.com Ltd

THE BARBARA CARTLAND PINK COLLECTION

Barbara Cartland was the most prolific bestselling author in the history of the world. She was frequently in the Guinness Book of Records for writing more books in a year than any other living author. In fact her most amazing literary feat was when her publishers asked for more Barbara Cartland romances, she doubled her output from 10 books a year to over 20 books a year, when she was 77.

She went on writing continuously at this rate for 20 years and wrote her last book at the age of 97, thus completing 400 books between the ages of 77 and 97.

Her publishers finally could not keep up with this phenomenal output, so at her death she left 160 unpublished manuscripts, something again that no other author has ever achieved.

Now the exciting news is that these 160 original unpublished Barbara Cartland books are already being published and by Barbaracartland.com exclusively on the internet, as the international web is the best possible way of reaching so many Barbara Cartland readers around the world.

The 160 books are published monthly and will be numbered in sequence.

The series is called the Pink Collection as a tribute to Barbara Cartland whose favourite colour was pink and it became very much her trademark over the years.

The Barbara Cartland Pink Collection is published only on the internet. Log on to www.barbaracartland.com to find out how you can purchase the books monthly as they are published, and take out a subscription that will ensure that all subsequent editions are delivered to you by mail order to your home.

NEW

Barbaracartland.com is proud to announce the publication of ten new Audio Books for the first time as CDs. They are favourite Barbara Cartland stories read by well-known actors and actresses and each story extends to 4 or 5 CDs. The Audio Books are as follows:

The Patient Bridegroom	The Passion and the Flower
A Challenge of Hearts	Little White Doves of Love
A Train to Love	The Prince and the Pekinese
The Unbroken Dream	A King in Love
The Cruel Count	A Sign of Love

More Audio Books will be published in the future and the above titles can be purchased by logging on to the website www.barbaracartland.com or please write to the address below.

If you do not have access to a computer, you can write for information about the Barbara Cartland Pink Collection and the Barbara Cartland Audio Books to the following address:

Barbara Cartland.com Ltd., Camfield Place,
Hatfield, Hertfordshire AL9 6JE, United Kingdom.

Telephone: +44 (0)1707 642629
Fax: +44 (0)1707 663041

THE LATE DAME BARBARA CARTLAND

Barbara Cartland who sadly died in May 2000 at the age of nearly 99 was the world's most famous romantic novelist who wrote 723 books in her lifetime with worldwide sales of over 1 billion copies and her books were translated into 36 different languages.

As well as romantic novels, she wrote historical biographies, 6 autobiographies, theatrical plays, books of advice on life, love, vitamins and cookery. She also found time to be a political speaker and television and radio personality.

She wrote her first book at the age of 21 and this was called *Jigsaw*. It became an immediate bestseller and sold 100,000 copies in hardback and was translated into 6 different languages. She wrote continuously throughout her life, writing bestsellers for an astonishing 76 years. Her books have always been immensely popular in the United States, where in 1976 her current books were at numbers 1 & 2 in the B. Dalton bestsellers list, a feat never achieved before or since by any author.

Barbara Cartland became a legend in her own lifetime and will be best remembered for her wonderful romantic novels, so loved by her millions of readers throughout the world.

Her books will always be treasured for their moral message, her pure and innocent heroines, her good looking and dashing heroes and above all her belief that the power of love is more important than anything else in everyone's life.

"I have often been asked by both men and women as to how do you know when you are really in love and it is not just plain infatuation.

My answer is always the same.

You are in love when your loved one is never out of your mind for a single second day or night and in addition you just cannot bear to wait until you see and touch her or him again."

Barbara Cartland

CHAPTER ONE
1872

A bearded and disreputable figure in the tattered dress of a Muslim Holy man moved into the deserted cave with a sigh of relief.

He had been walking for miles and was desperately tired.

At the same time he knew that he had to climb out of sight before he was observed.

He looked around the large cave.

He realised that if he climbed to the far end of it, he would not only be well out of sight, but above the people coming after him who he wanted to overhear.

He was, in fact, a British officer – Captain David Ingle of the Sixth Bengal Native Cavalry Regiment.

Like many other Officers he had joined what at the time was the most exciting but dangerous Secret Service in the whole world.

During the last twelve years the British had realised that the Russians were expanding and taking over the small Caravan towns and the Muslim Khanates that lay between their Southern border and the frontier of Northern India.

One by one they were falling to the Cossacks, who always spearheaded the advance of the Russian troops.

The Russians were now creeping closer and closer to India's still weakly guarded North-West Frontier.

In 1865 the great walled City of Tashkent had been forced to submit humbly to the Czar and three years later it was the turn of Samarkand and Bokhara.

Despite the Czar's repeated assurances that he and the Russians did not have hostile intentions towards India, the British both at home and in India were becoming more and more concerned.

It was known that several of the Czar's most able Generals had already drawn up a plan of invasion.

In recent years it had been only '*The Great Game*' that attempted to contain this dangerous threat.

This peril had intensified as more and more young Officers were prepared to risk their lives – in fact quite a number of them had already died.

They undertook increasingly dangerous journeys in disguise to report on Russian movements as well as to try to win over the allegiance of weak and suspicious Khans.

A large number of the players in this strange secret struggle were professionals – Indian Army Officers and the political Agents sent by their superiors in Calcutta to seek for information of every kind.

The amateurs were, as it happened, no less capable.

It was openly repeated that *The Great Game* was much too perilous for Europeans and yet it was they who explored and mapped those parts of Southern Asia which had to be surveyed if India was to be effectively defended.

Thus disguised as Muslim Holy men and Buddhist pilgrims they had succeeded in secretly mapping thousands of square acres of previously unexplored territory.

David Ingle had jumped at the chance of joining *The Great Game* and this had come just a year after he had proved himself an excellent soldier and was on the list of young Officers selected for early promotion.

He had the reputation for being extremely lucky and he brought information back to Headquarters that they had never been able to obtain through anyone else.

For him it was an excitement he enjoyed more than anything else.

He had been clever enough to learn to speak Urdu fluently and he had learnt sufficient Russian to understand what his enemies were saying, this was if he was fortunate or unfortunate enough to be in contact with them.

From what he had seen and heard on his missions, he was even more convinced than the Viceroy himself that India was in great danger.

It required intense planning and far more attention than those at home were giving it if India was to be saved.

Now he climbed up to the roof of the cave.

And as he did so, he was well aware that if he was discovered, he would undoubtedly die.

Worse still he could be tortured before his head was finally chopped from his body.

He had been recruited to watch the Russian Cavalry who were infiltrating over the country further North.

It was then that he became concerned with what was happening at Fort Tibbee, a fort on India's North-West Frontier – it was named after a village that had originally stood there before the Frontier became a battleground.

David had been on a mission that had taken him to several small independent States, lying to the North-West collectively known as Sind.

It was in Sind he formed a suspicion that something sinister was being planned against Fort Tibbee, although it was little more than an intuition.

So instead of moving on to his intended destination, he had hastily doubled back.

Now he was in sight of Tibbee and he could see the British flag flying over the Fort.

He was certain that as everything seemed quiet, the garrison had not the slightest idea that anything unusual was likely to happen.

There was one lesson that David had learnt in his many years of serving in *The Great Game*, and that was nothing was more dangerous than when the British Army thought themselves safe and were not looking for trouble.

It was then that the Russians would send in a more formidable force, usually Cossacks, riding brilliantly and they would lead the way and even command the respect of their enemies.

David recognised that their equipment, training and morale were remarkable.

Even he had been astonished by the hardiness of the Cossacks, who slept out in the snow in midwinter without tents and apparently were not perturbed by any obstacle.

As a Cavalry Officer he was exceedingly impressed by the feat of one particular Regiment of Cossacks, which had captured an enemy Fortress by galloping into it before the defenders could close the gates.

That was sheer drama, but the Russians were clever enough to infiltrate their spies and their agents among the Indians themselves and particularly among the tribesmen.

These fierce tribesmen, who hated any nationality other than their own, could be incited into making trouble.

They were easily bribed to harass the British forces, who they believed had no right to be in their country.

So the British always had to be on their guard that small uprisings amongst the people could take place at any time and on any pretext.

The Russians exploited every situation and sent in,

as they had in the Balkans, men to stir up trouble and foster revolution where it was least expected.

David had overheard a whispered sentence he was not supposed to hear and it had made him alert.

The North-West Frontier had always been a bone of contention between the tribesmen and the British Army.

The tribesmen resented any Fort built on land they considered theirs and British Officers ordering them about and expecting their orders to be obeyed.

Thus, having changed his plans, David had made for Fort Tibbee.

It had been a very hard and uncomfortable journey and he was by this time extremely tired.

And the Fort was now in sight and it was his duty to convince those inside to be more on their guard.

He realised that it was always difficult in the heat of India and when there was nothing very much happening to keep men alert and ready to fight at a moment's notice.

Having spent several days in a large Fort soon after arriving in India, he had learnt how very difficult it was for every man from the Commanding Officer down to the most recent recruit.

He had heard the word 'cave' in a conversation that had alerted him and he had known instinctively that meant the cave where he was now hiding.

It was a large cave and was appreciated by anyone sleeping out on the mountain as it was a protection against the hot sun in summer and the winds and snows of winter.

As he climbed as high as he could in the cave and realised that he could go no further, he was hoping that he would not fall asleep.

It was certainly a danger, since he had walked all through the night and had only come within sight of Fort Tibbee as dawn was breaking.

Disguised as a Muslim Holy man, he knew that he would be safe amongst the tribesmen.

At the same time to be among them was to waste a great deal of time as they would ask him for his blessing, kneeling down in front of him to receive it and if he was not careful, they would tell him all their personal troubles.

It was therefore only by running for the last mile or so before dawn broke that he had been able to reach the cave without being seen and as he slipped into it, he had said a prayer of thankfulness that it was unoccupied.

He could thus do what he intended and hide among the rocks where he could hear but not be seen and he had achieved this, but not without tearing his already ragged garments.

His notebook, containing all the information he had gleaned with so much difficulty during the past month, was slightly torn.

However, he was now well hidden in the cave and all he had to do was to wait.

Despite his resolution not to fall asleep, his eyelids were drooping and his limbs became relaxed.

Suddenly, he heard two men enter the cave below him and instantly with the acuteness of someone who has faced danger a dozen times, David was instantly vigilant.

Then as the man below spoke he drew in his breath, hearing that he was a Russian.

"I suppose they'll turn up," the Russian grunted in a thick voice.

"You can be sure of that," the other man answered.

He did not speak again.

But David was aware that they had sat down on one of the flat stones which provided the only place they could sit on except on the rough floor itself.

Then he heard that they were eating and as his own stomach was empty, he remembered that he had not eaten for a long time.

The Russians ate noisily, belching occasionally, but not speaking.

Then just like a wave breaking on a stony beach the cave was suddenly filled with tribesmen.

It seemed as if they all entered in a rush and David guessed that there were twelve or more of them.

For twenty minutes he could hardly breathe as with every nerve in his body he listened to what was being said, thanking God that they were speaking in Urdu which he was familiar with.

They were taking instructions from the Russians, who, like he, had taken the trouble to learn the language of the tribesmen.

Their orders were quite simple.

They were to attack the Fort at dawn the next day and be very careful meanwhile to keep out of sight so that the British inside would not realise that they were even in the vicinity.

As he listened and continued listening, David could not help but being impressed by the way the Russians gave their orders.

They had clearly thought out every detail and made it absolutely clear to the tribesmen what they were to do and how they were to do it.

They were planning to overpower the Garrison of Fort Tibbee by sheer weight of numbers.

"You must kill every man before they kill you," the Russian was saying. "And if you're lucky, which I believe you will be, most of the men in the Fort will be asleep."

He looked round him before continuing,

"Those on guard must be overpowered before they can shoot and raise the alarm. Kill every man and when you've succeeded, clear out of the Fort and go back to your villages before reinforcements can arrive. Then they will not know who has attacked the Fort or on whom they can avenge themselves."

The tribesmen clearly understood.

One or two asked questions, but on the whole they seemed happy with the Russian plan and were prepared to carry it out without seeing any particular difficulties.

David knew that they had used just the same tactics many times before.

As in the case of Forts that were overrun before the gates could be closed, there had been many cruel murders and assassinations for which no one had an explanation.

As swiftly and stealthily as they had appeared, the tribesmen left, leaving a trail of destruction behind them.

They were never very talkative, as David knew, and the two Russians were clever enough not to overload their minds.

They had been given their orders and simply told when and how to attack the Fort and to lie low until the very last moment.

When the tribesmen had gone, one of the Russians enquired to the other in his own language,

"Do you think they understood?"

"I'll answer that question tomorrow evening," the other Russian responded, "but we've been quite successful with these tribesmen in the past."

"That's true and the Czar's been saying, I believe, that while we have done well in Southern Asia, we've not made much impact on India so far."

The other man gave a laugh.

"I thought that he was keeping that one for the end, when he adds India to the Russian Empire!"

Listening to every word, David clenched his fists.

For a good long time the Russian Empire had been steadily expanding at the rate of fifty-five square miles a day and he reckoned that this made over twenty thousand square miles a year.

He remembered a statement he had heard at one of many meetings at Government House in Calcutta.

A Senior Officer had said that at the beginning of the nineteenth century over two thousand miles separated the Russian Empire from the British in Asia.

Yet now he knew – although few liked to think of it – it had shrunk to just a few hundred miles.

David drew in his breath.

He knew, as did so many in *The Great Game*, that the aggressive Cossacks would only rein in their mounts when India was theirs.

At present he did not even want to think about it.

What he had to do now was to sneak into the Fort without being suspected by the tribesmen.

It was still some way away and he was well aware that there were tribesmen lying hidden amongst the rocks and the shrubs, preparing themselves for the onslaught just before dawn the next day.

He waited for twenty minutes after the Russians left the cave, as he knew only too well that he had to be quite certain they were well out of sight before he appeared.

Men had too often lost their lives for coming out of hiding too early – someone could come back for something he had left behind.

The sun had risen while David was still in the cave and it almost blinded him as he climbed slowly down.

He pulled his tattered garment into place – it had served its purpose well and he would need no excuse for buying a new one. Then adjusting his headgear he brushed a hand over his beard, which made him seem far older than he was.

He moved out of the cave and into the open.

There was no sign of anyone and yet he knew they were undoubtedly out there amongst the rocks in the high grass or sleeping peacefully without worrying themselves about what lay ahead.

Slowly, very slowly, as it was always a mistake to seem to be in a hurry, he moved in the direction of the Fort.

He opened the Holy Book he carried in his pocket.

Anyone who saw him would think he was engaged in Morning Prayer which is compulsory for Muslims.

If he thought anyone was suspicious of him, he was ready to go down on his knees and pray.

There had been many occasions when this had not been a pretence, when he had been praying desperately that he would not be discovered and that he would survive.

His prayers had always been answered, but today he recognised that it had never been more important that he should reach Fort Tibbee in time.

It would be a bad mistake to appear to be heading directly to the Fort, so he therefore made a detour passing some men lying beneath some bushes.

They raised themselves to ask for his blessing and David gave it to them.

He was word perfect in what he was supposed to say having been taught by a Muslim Imam and he had also listened to a genuine Holy man addressing his flock.

He was fully aware of what he should say in answer to their requests.

During the many journeys he had undertaken in this particular disguise no one had ever been suspicious of him.

He had acquired a large amount of information that was desperately needed by those in command of the Army in India.

He was now moving nearer and nearer to the Fort.

As he did so, David was aware that in every small place of cover tribesmen were arriving in order to conceal themselves.

They were coming in twos and threes, but they kept on coming and he began to think that, however many men there were in the Fort, they would be outnumbered by the enemy outside.

He was desperately hungry and exceedingly thirsty in the heat of the sun, but he thought it would be a mistake to stop for any length of time or linger for too long to talk to the tribesmen who spoke to him.

As he had learnt in his many years of service, just one faulty word or one uneasy movement could make the enemy suspicious.

If he was on edge, the tribesmen were too, thinking about what they had to do before dawn the next day.

On and on he shuffled, walking in the almost limp manner of a tired elderly man.

As he grew nearer and nearer to the Fort, he could see there were just a few soldiers moving about with most of them obviously following the Indian habit of enjoying a long siesta at midday.

There were a number of bushy shrubs growing not far from the main gate and David sat down in their shade, crossing his legs Indian style and bending his head as if he was concerned only with his prayers.

The gates of the Fort were closed and he could only

wait and hope that they would soon be opened to receive a visitor or one of their own Officers.

It was over two hours later when he could see two horsemen followed by a detachment of soldiers coming up the side of an adjacent hill.

They were, he thought, some Officers calling on the Colonel or perhaps they were carrying a message from the powers that be.

It would be dangerous, as David well knew, for the Officers to ride alone without an escort.

It was a regular joke that behind every stone on the North-West Frontier there was an enemy waiting to take a potshot at you.

Sadly it was true and David knew that the Officers, although they appeared at ease, were acutely conscious that at any moment a rifle might be fired at them.

To reach the path that led to the main gates of the Fort they would have to pass by him.

Slowly he rose to his feet.

Then, as the Officers rode towards him, he held out his hand.

"Help the poor, Sahib. Help those who are hungry. Help those who are ill."

He was speaking exactly in the sing-song voice of an Indian beggar.

As the Officers were completely ignoring him, he ran beside their horses, calling out again and again,

"Help, Sahibs, please help and you will be blessed by Allah for your kindness."

Those watching from the Fort had seen the Officers approaching and the gates swung open.

As the horsemen rode into the Fort, David followed closely behind them.

He was well inside before the Sergeant of the guard saw him.

"*You*," he called out, "get out of 'ere!"

The Sergeant walked menacingly towards him.

As he reached him, David said in English,

"Take me immediately to your Colonel – "

The Sergeant stared at him.

By this time the two Officers had rode on and were dismounting as two soldiers ran to their horses' heads.

"Close the gate now," David ordered the Sergeant. "Bolt it and then take me to the Colonel at once."

The Sergeant was obviously astonished, but equally he was aware that despite his extraordinary appearance the man speaking to him was English – and he was giving him orders in the same manner that a British Officer would do.

David pulled off his headgear and smoothed back his greasy hair.

He was tired, very tired, but he had achieved what he had set out to accomplish and this at least gave him a small glow of satisfaction.

The Sergeant had told the guard to shut the gate and now he was back again at David's side.

"Who are you?" he demanded aggressively.

"That is my business, Sergeant. Now do as I told you and hurry about it. There is no time to be lost."

Bewildered yet feeling he could not refuse to obey him, the Sergeant walked ahead.

The two Officers, unaware of what had occurred, had already disappeared and their escort were chatting with a small group of soldiers.

David could hear them laughing and no one had the slightest idea that he had achieved a minor victory in *The Great Game* by getting himself into the Fort unsuspected.

He was led along various passages until they came to what David recognised were the Officers' quarters.

The Sergeant stopped outside a door, knocked and then he turned to David,

"Now stay 'ere, while I tell the Colonel about you."

He opened the door and David pushed past him.

Colonel Jones was seated at his writing desk and he looked up in astonishment at the figure confronting him.

David raised his hand in salute.

"Captain David Ingle reporting, sir!"

"Good God!" exclaimed the Colonel. "I suppose as you are in disguise, you are on some mission."

"Exactly, sir, and I have something of the greatest importance to tell you and it cannot wait."

The Colonel pointed to a chair on the other side of his desk.

"Sit down, Captain, and I suppose, if you have been travelling in this heat, you would like something to drink."

"I would be most grateful, sir. I have had nothing to eat or drink for the last three days."

The Colonel rang a bell on his desk and the door opened immediately.

"Food and drink," he ordered the servant who had appeared, "and be quick about it."

As the servant closed the door, the Colonel turned to David, wiping his forehead with his hand.

"What is this all about, Captain?"

"You are going to be attacked in strength at dawn. Tribesmen are already collecting from every direction and I think, in the Russians' eyes, it will be a major assault. If they can take this Fort, it would be a feather in their cap."

The Colonel was listening to David carefully.

He picked up another bell and rang it vigorously.

At once the door opened and an Officer appeared.

"You rang, sir?"

"I want every Officer and the Sergeant Major here immediately," Colonel Jones barked out.

The Officer's eyes widened and then, as he looked at David in astonishment, he replied,

"I will send those who have not heard the bell, sir."

As he turned, three more Officers came hurrying in to the room.

The Colonel introduced them all to David and then told them to bring in some chairs.

While they were doing so, the servant came back with a tray of food and a bottle of Indian beer. He set the tray down on the side of the desk and David began to eat.

He was experienced enough to eat slowly, knowing that to gobble when one was starving was a grave mistake.

The Colonel did not speak to him and he ate with a sense of relief and only as he finished the last drop of beer did he realise that the room was now filled.

The Officers were all seated on the chairs and the Sergeant-Major was standing against the wall.

David looked up at the Colonel and smiled.

"Thank you very much, sir, I have never enjoyed a meal more!"

The Colonel laughed.

"You will have another as soon as you have told us why you are here and why it is so urgent."

David turned his chair around so that he was facing the Officers in the room.

"You must forgive me," he began, "if I sit whilst I am talking, but I have been walking for what has seemed to me an age and my feet are somewhat tired."

He then informed them of what he had overheard in the cave, explaining in detail that he was there because of something he had heard in one of the local villages.

Because the Officers suspected that he was in *The Great Game*, they listened to every word attentively and only when he had finished did they ply him with questions.

He thought it only right to inform them about how close the Russians were to them and the devastation they were causing among the Khanates and the Caravan towns.

Finally the Colonel took over.

"You have heard what Captain Ingle has told us and I will now tell you what we must do."

The Officers looked up at him as he continued,

"We must wipe out the attackers before they reach the Fort. After midnight tonight every man who can use a rifle must be ready to shoot – not on sight, as you may not see them until they are on top of us but at every movement. Even though it is dark, you will be aware of a man moving towards the Fort, whether he is walking or on his stomach. It is absolutely essential that not one of them gain access."

"I should imagine, sir, they will be carrying some means of breaking down the gates."

"I have thought of that, Napier. They will not only be doubly strengthened but heavily guarded."

"I am certain that's very wise, sir. Shall we go now and set up the barriers?"

David gave a cry of protest.

"They are watching the Fort from every available tree or even from a distant rock or hillock. Nothing should be moved, and you should not give them the slightest idea that you are anticipating trouble?"

As an afterthought he added,

"Is that not correct, sir?"

He thought that perhaps the Colonel would resent his taking over.

"You are so right, Captain. Everything must appear entirely normal. Moreover one can never be quite certain that they do not have sympathisers inside the Fort."

David sighed.

"So true, sir. It has happened before and at the cost of many Britisish lives."

"What we must do is relatively simple. Every rifle, every pistol has to be loaded and ready. But to all intents and purposes we are walking in the sunshine unperturbed, having not the slightest idea of what might happen. Is that, Captain Ingle, what you think is the right tactic?"

"It is the *only* tactic, sir."

David rose a little unsteadily to his feet.

"May I rest for just two or three hours, sir?"

"Of course. Of course," Colonel Jones agreed as if he should have thought of it himself.

He told one of the Officers to take him to his room where he knew there was a second bed.

"Let him sleep, but wake the Captain before dinner which we will have a little later than usual."

David smiled.

"I shall look forward to dinner, sir."

Major Atkins led him from the Colonel's office.

Only as they walked down the passage did David hear a burst of noise behind him and he guessed that every Officer had started talking all at once.

Major Atkins' room was comparatively cool and the bed was comfortable.

At that moment David would have slept on a bed of nails and not been aware of it.

He threw off his tattered robe, kicked off his shoes, lay down and was fast asleep before his head touched the pillow.

Major Atkins shaded the window from the sun and then left the room closing the door quietly behind him.

He then joined the turmoil upstairs realising that his brother Officers were all excited at the idea of action.

Life could be seriously dull in a Fort where nothing happened day after day. There were few amusements and certainly not an attractive woman anywhere.

As the Colonel had ordered, weapons were put at the ready and at the same time only inside the buildings of the Fort was there any sign of activity.

Outside men walked about casually as they always did and looked out over the magnificent view, but took no particular interest in it.

David had slept for over four hours without moving when he was woken for dinner.

A bath was prepared for him and he shaved away his beard and the Major lent him some decent clothes.

"I apologise for being a nuisance, Major."

"You are not a nuisance at all."

The Major tried, however, to draw David out into telling him where he had been and what he had done.

But David knew it was always a mistake as it might make things difficult for those who followed him, because of something he had said, they might be caught and killed.

It was a wise provision in *The Great Game* that no one, as far as possible, would know who else was in it and every player was referred to only by a number.

David could only hope that the Officers and men of Fort Tibbee would not talk when they went on leave.

Otherwise as he was now known to all of them to be in *The Great Game*, it would make everything he tried to do in the future a thousand times more difficult and very much more dangerous.

'I will speak to them tomorrow,' he told himself.

Then he went to the Officer's Mess for dinner.

Because Indian servants were present, they talked about sport and the political situation in Calcutta – the new Viceroy, Lord Mayo, had been welcomed by all with much enthusiasm when he had arrived and he was proving to be an exceptional leader.

When dinner was finished, they all moved into the room where the Officers always congregated after dinner, where there were several card tables set out.

"Play as we usually do," the Colonel ordered all the Officers and sat down at one of the tables himself.

David settled himself in an armchair and before he could be bombarded with more questions he fell asleep and after what they had heard, no one dared to wake him.

It was midnight before the Colonel rose from his card table,

"I suggest you now change your clothes and go on duty. Dawn is early, as we all know, and we should be in our proper places well before four o'clock."

The Officers then all left the room and the Colonel was left with Major Atkins and David was still fast asleep in the armchair.

"Shall I wake him, sir?" the Major asked.

The Colonel shook his head.

"No, let him sleep on. I know just how it feels to be on edge for many days and only sleep can make up for what he has been through."

"When shall I wake him, sir?"

"Just before you come on duty and give him a rifle and a revolver, if he wants one."

They both left the room and David slept on.

It was an hour later that he awoke with a start and instantly alert, he sensed danger.

Major Atkins told him,

"We are going on duty now. The Colonel said you are to have a rifle and a revolver – they are beside you."

"I have been asleep?" asked David in surprise.

"You deserved it, Captain."

"I will only have deserved it if everything turns out as we hope."

David picked up the rifle.

"Now where do you want me to go?"

"Where else but with the Colonel in the front line, and I will take you there."

Major Atkins walked ahead.

David rubbed his eyes.

'I hope when this is all over,' he thought to himself, 'I will be able to sleep the clock round.'

Then he wondered that if after all the planning, the Russians might just prevail and Fort Tibbee would fall into their hands.

This of course would mean disaster for the garrison, but much worse, it would be a deadly blow at British India.

David drew in his breath in trepidation.

'We *must* win this battle,' he determined, 'and with God's help we will.'

CHAPTER TWO

It was so splendid, David mused triumphantly later, how everything had gone according to plan.

The soldiers crept into their positions and when he had appeared, the Colonel asked him to stand beside him.

All they could see faintly in the moonlight was the empty hillsides around them.

Then when the men were all in position, there was a poignant silence that combined with the hush that always comes before dawn.

To David it was as if the world drew in its breath.

Suddenly there was a faint movement in some thick grass and just a suspicion of shadows moving from behind rocks in the distance.

Every man at his post, wherever he was, stiffened.

It was impossible not to sense the thrill that every soldier knows so well before he goes into action.

The moon was fading fast and the stars were going out one by one.

Now David could discern faint movements coming nearer and nearer towards the Fort.

On the Colonel's orders no one moved an inch and there was still an overwhelming silence.

Suddenly as if on an unseen and unheard command, the front line of the enemy rose to their feet and started to run quickly towards the gates of the Fort.

As they took their first step the Colonel barked out, "*Fire!*"

The noise of the rifles seemed to strike the air.

The first line of advancing tribesmen hesitated and then when those behind them started to move forward, they bumped into them as they were not moving.

As tribesmen began to fall, the others dithered.

Now the British soldiers were firing at them again and again and the enemy were falling one after another.

It was then the rearmost of the attackers panicked – they turned back and started to run.

As soon as they did so, those who had been in front of them and were still alive followed.

On the Colonel's orders the British soldiers went on firing and only when the last of the enemy was out of range did he give the order to cease fire.

He turned and put his hand on David's shoulder.

"We have won the battle, thanks to your warning, Captain Ingle, and we are all very grateful."

It was some time before the tribesmen came back to collect their dead. At first they crawled up apprehensively and then as they were ignored, they came more boldly and carried the bodies away.

Watching them from the Fort, David thought it was unlikely that any of the wounded would live for long.

It was a complete failure that would infuriate the Russians, but there was nothing that they could do about it.

He was also certain, as was the Colonel when they discussed it, that having failed at Fort Tibbee, the Russians would not try again in a hurry – at any rate not with the same tribesmen, who they would now no longer trust.

"I am writing a full report," the Colonel told David,

"to the Commander-in-Chief in Calcutta, who will then, of course, convey it to the Viceroy."

"I would take it myself, sir, but I am going to ask if I may stay here for a day or two to ease my feet. Walking for three days without sleeping was bad enough, but these Muslim sandals of are not the best footwear for extremely rough mountain paths."

The Colonel was most sympathetic and he was also delighted to have David as his guest – he learnt much from him about the current situation over the border in Asia.

He was worried, as all Commanding Officers were, about Russian expansion, which had been achieved above all thanks to the remarkable work of the Cossacks.

David enjoyed a short rest at the Fort, but he knew that he must return to his Regiment.

"I only hope," the Colonel remarked to him when they were alone, "that they will not want you to take on another mission in *The Great Game* as soon as you return. But you have been so successful so far that I fear they will be reluctant to let you rest on your laurels."

"I do enjoy the work, Colonel, although sometimes I am amazed to find that I am still alive the next morning!"

The Colonel laughed.

"India is deeply in your debt, Captain, and of those of your contemporaries who are playing the same game."

"I only hope," David responded seriously, "that the Government at home in England will realise that we must have more Regiments and more equipment sent to India."

"I think that you can trust Lord Mayo to tell them so. He has, I am told, more commonsense than any other Viceroy we have ever had."

David thought that this was true, and on his return to Calcutta, which took him well over a week, he was in fact thinking about the Earl of Mayo.

He was realising, as a number of others were doing, that he was exactly what India needed.

When Mr. Disraeli, the Prime Minister, appointed him, he was guided by his intuition.

It had seemed extraordinary to most of the Cabinet that a forty-six year old Irish Peer should be chosen for one of the most elevated but difficult positions in the Empire.

The House of Commons had called it an eccentric choice, whilst many others complained that his experience has been entirely in Ireland and had been rude about him.

Actually, as David knew, after nearly two years in office, the majority, especially those in India, realised that his appointment had been a stroke of genius.

Lord Mayo was the Head of an ancient Norman-Irish clan. He had played only a minor part in politics and had distinguished himself more than in any other way by being an outstanding Master of the Kildare Hunt.

Why this should qualify him for his appointment as Viceroy of India had seemed ridiculous at the time.

Tall, broad-shouldered and powerfully built, he was a splendid figure of a man and he showed determination and humour in his clean-shaven face.

Almost as soon as he arrived in India as Viceroy his enthusiasm, gaiety and kindness of heart contributed to a personal magnetism that few could resist.

Benjamin Disraeli had appreciated that having lived through the 'hungry forties' in Ireland, he would bring to the famine-ridden land of India his first-hand experience of dealing with hunger in its most horrifying aspect.

During the Irish famine Lord Mayo had worked for the relief of suffering, spending long hours riding from one stricken area to another.

This experience had well prepared him for what he

was to encounter in India and had made him understanding and sympathetic in a way that would have been impossible for other ordinary men.

As he had a quick grasp of any problem, he realised soon after his arrival the significance of *The Great Game*.

He had made it abundantly clear that he wished to know exactly what was happening and to meet, whenever possible, those who were taking part in it.

*

David travelled to Calcutta using many different kinds of conveyance and finally by train.

He thought as he did so that the Viceroy would be exceedingly pleased that by a miracle he had been able to save Fort Tibbee.

No one knew better than he did what would have happened if he had not arrived when he had and warned the Colonel – the tribesmen and Russians would undoubtedly by now have killed or taken prisoner the whole garrison and then they would have destroyed the Fort itself.

When David reached Calcutta, he went at once to report to the Colonel of his Regiment, who as he expected, sent him straight to Government House.

He never went there without appreciating the great beauty of it.

Government House dominated Calcutta in a way no other building had ever done.

Anything he told the Viceroy was secret even from his secretaries and *aides-de-camp*.

The Viceroy had been given the time of David's arrival before he left Regimental Headquarters.

He arrived exactly on the time appointed and was taken by an Indian servant wearing an elaborate red and white uniform to the Viceroy's private study.

25

It was well-known that Lord Mayo rose very early and this enabled him to get through a large amount of work without sacrificing time for exercise or his night's sleep.

When David was shown into his room, the Viceroy was seated at a writing desk in front of the open windows.

He looked up and there was no doubt that he was genuinely pleased to see David.

He rose and held out his hand.

"I am delighted to see you, Captain Ingle. I know you have brought with you some good news and I want to hear every detail of what occurred at Fort Tibbee."

He walked from his writing desk and indicated a comfortable chair in front of an open window.

"Now tell me everything from the very beginning. I am exceedingly interested in what you have discovered in the lands North of the frontier and I am very worried about the continued advance of the Russians."

David knew that he had every reason to be so, and did not spare any detail from his story.

He emphasised that in his opinion the British were not giving enough support to the Khanates and small towns lying to the North – in consequence they were forced to capitulate far too quickly to the Cossacks.

The Viceroy listened intently to every word, only occasionally did he interrupt to ask an intelligent question.

David talked on, until he finished with the battle at Fort Tibbee.

He told the Viceroy that only two British soldiers had been slightly wounded whilst the enemy dead must, he thought, be little short of a thousand.

"I can only add my gratitude, Captain, to those who have already thanked you. I find it amazing that you were clever enough to understand that Tibbee was in danger and managed to reach there in time to prevent what could quite easily have been a massacre."

"It was a long walk, Your Excellency, which I do not wish to make again, but I think it is important that the Forts on the North-West Frontier should be strengthened and their garrison augmented."

"I agree with you and it is a priority I will discuss with those in command immediately."

David thought that his audience was at an end and he was expecting to rise to his feet when the Viceroy said,

"And now Captain, I have news for you which I am afraid you will find rather upsetting."

David looked at him in surprise.

"*News*, Your Excellency?"

"A cable has come through from England. As you were away it was brought to me, but it was impossible for anyone to be in touch with you, as we had no idea where you were. You are therefore receiving it now, nearly three weeks after it was originally despatched."

David was wondering what the cable could possibly contain.

The Viceroy handed it to him and he saw that it was addressed to him at Regimental Headquarters.

He was surprised that they should have bothered the Viceroy with his cable.

Then he read,

"*Deepest regrets to have to inform you that your grandfather, the Marquis of Inglestone and his heir, the Viscount Stone, were killed yesterday when the carriage carrying them over the bridge in the Park lost a wheel.*

Their Lordships were thrown into the stream which was in spate and as they fell their heads crashed into the bridge's brick piers and they were knocked unconscious.

It was impossible to save either of them before they were drowned.

The funeral will take place on Saturday and, as you are next of kin to your grandfather, you inherit his title and Ingle Hall and we await your Lordship's instructions.

Yours faithfully

Turnbull, Downside and Mellow."

David read it through with astonishment, realising from the signature at the end that the cable was from his grandfather's Solicitors.

Then the Viceroy added sympathetically,

"I am sorry, Ingle, that this should have happened to spoil what should be your most glorious hour, although, of course, that has to be kept secret."

"Whatever can I do now?" asked David, speaking almost more to himself than to the Viceroy.

"I am afraid that you will have to go home, we will miss you, but in the circumstances it must be a wise course to take. If the Russians by some means get to know that you are responsible for their disaster at Fort Tibbee, you would be safer, to say the least of it, well out of India."

"But I have no wish to go, Your Excellency, I want to stay with the Regiment – "

"And, of course," added the Viceroy, "in *The Great Game*. But as I have already said, I think at the moment it would be extremely dangerous for you."

David recognised that he was talking sensibly, but at the same time he was finding it hard to believe that his life in India had unexpectedly come to such an abrupt end.

As if he could divine David's thoughts, the Viceroy advised,

"Captain, you are now, I understand, the Marquis of Inglestone. It will undoubtedly mean many problems for

28

you to solve and a great many people who will look to you for help and succour."

He smiled before he continued,

"You will find much of what you have learnt in *The Great Game* will give you valuable assistance in your new life, if nothing else."

David drew in a deep breath.

He had never in his wildest dreams believed that he could ever inherit his grandfather's title and be the owner of Ingle Hall, the ancient family home.

When his father, Lord Richard Ingle, left England, the Marquis was an exceedingly active man and at sixty-seven he was strong for his age.

His elder son by his first marriage, Viscount Stone, was in contrast somewhat of a weakling and although he was then over thirty, he had never married.

David had had his difficulties, but he had failed to elicit any help from his grandfather at a time of great need.

"I do appreciate," the Viceroy was saying, "that this has given you a great shock. And, of course, I need not say how India will miss you and so will I personally. But I am afraid, Captain, you must leave for home immediately."

"*Immediately*?" David echoed in surprise.

"Because I think it is for your own safety as well as what will be expected of you by your family at home. I have actually booked a cabin for you on the P & O Steamer leaving here tonight."

David stared at the Viceroy.

"Tonight – " he muttered.

He was finding it hard to take in first what the cable had told him and secondly the Viceroy's attitude.

As if the Viceroy thought he must explain, he said,

"I have had, as I expect you know, a report from the Colonel at Tibbee telling me how you saved the Fort and undoubtedly his life as well as that of the garrison."

David made a murmur, but he did not interrupt.

"He described, in rather more detail than you have done, the devastation you caused among the tribesmen and I gather from a further report which reached me yesterday that there were a number of Russians among the dead."

He paused before he continued,

"This, as you know better than I do, is something they will not forget and which they will be determined to avenge. I therefore think it important for you and for your family that you should return to England at once."

"Of course I must depart," agreed David, "if Your Excellency believes that I cannot stay usefully, as I would really like to."

"If the Russians avenged themselves against you, it would cause much consternation not only in Calcutta but in the Ingle family in England and in those who live on your grandfather's estate."

David parted his lips to say something and then he changed his mind and remained silent.

"As you may know, I have not spent much time in England before coming here," the Viceroy went on, "but I know that the Marquis of Inglestone had a position of great significance and as the new Marquis you will be expected to carry on his duties where he has had to leave off."

"Actually the situation will be rather different, but if Your Excellency insists, I must go back to England. But I assure you, I would much rather remain in India, however dangerous such a decision might be."

"As you are far too valuable to us, Captain, to be wiped out quite unnecessarily, I must insist on you saving yourself. I intend to ask Her Majesty the Queen to honour you as you well deserve for what you have done for India."

There was nothing David could do but thank him, so without saying anything further, he bowed himself out.

Only when he was outside Government House did he realise almost as if he was coming out of a trance that he was now the *Marquis of Inglestone*.

Now, although it seemed so incredible, he was in a position to propose to the girl he was deeply in love with.

He was penniless apart from his Army pay.

In his precarious life in *The Great Game* there was always a chance of his having no future and he had not told Stella Ashworth how much she meant to him.

He had kissed her gently when they were in Simla together, when he had called in to see her the night before setting off across the frontier in disguise.

He had not, of course, told her what he was doing – he had merely said he had been sent North by the Colonel of his Regiment and hoped he would not be away too long.

"I will miss you, David," she had purred softly.

"And I will miss you more than I dare tell you."

Stella looked at him with her large beautiful eyes.

He had swept her into his arms – he had always known that she was divinely desirable, but now she meant more to him than any woman he had ever met.

He kissed her until they were both breathless and then because he knew time was passing, he murmured,

"I must leave you now, my darling one, but when I come back I will have a great deal to say to you."

"Don't be away long, David," she pleaded. "You know that I love being with you, and you dance better than anyone else in the whole of Calcutta – "

David laughed.

"Is that so important?" he asked.

"It is to me and I just love dancing with you."

David had kissed her again.

Then as time was passing he had to hurry away to catch the night-train to carry him towards his target.

*

Now his brain had cleared a little after the shock of hearing of his grandfather's death.

He told himself that he was at least in a position to now ask Stella to be his wife.

As a General's daughter she lived in great comfort, and her father, David had always understood, had a private fortune, so he was better housed and could entertain in a way that none of his brother Officers could afford.

The General's grand house in Calcutta was one of the most outstanding in the City and it was certainly not provided for him by the Army.

When David raised the silver knocker on the door it was opened by an Indian servant wearing a smart livery.

He enquired if Miss Ashworth was at home and it was with a sense of relief he learned that she was indeed, and although she was expecting guests, there was no one with her at this moment.

David followed the servant upstairs to the drawing room, which boasted huge French windows overlooking a flower-filled garden.

When he entered the drawing room, it was to find Stella sitting on the sofa with her legs up reading a book.

As he was announced, she threw her book onto the floor and jumped to her feet.

"David!" she exclaimed. "You are back! Oh, how wonderful! I have been desperate at not hearing from you, and terribly afraid that you were in trouble or engaged in a battle with those horrible Russians."

David did not answer.

He merely put out his arms and pulled her close.

"Wherever I have been, Stella, I have missed you and this – "

His lips were on hers.

As he felt her respond, he thought nothing could be more marvellous or more exciting.

When he raised his head, he said in a deep voice,

"I adore you and you look even more beautiful than when I went away."

"Oh, David, I have missed you so very much, but now you are back we can enjoy ourselves again."

David looked down at her lovely face and then he mumbled,

"How soon will you marry me, my darling?"

He thought that Stella would move even closer, but instead to his astonishment, she replied,

"Oh, David, don't ask me that!"

"*Why not*?" David demanded sharply.

"Because," Stella said hesitatingly, "although I love you and enjoy being with you – I cannot marry you."

"Why Stella? I don't understand."

She moved closer and put her cheek against his.

"It sounds so horrid when I put it into words," she breathed in a voice he could hardly hear. "But I could not bear to marry a man who is poor and I know that my Papa would oppose our marriage even if I agreed to it."

"Why should he do so?"

"Oh, darling, you must be sensible about this. Papa wants me to marry someone important. He would prefer a man with a title, but he also wants my husband whoever he is to have enough money and that means quite a lot."

For a moment David was stunned into silence.

He just could not believe what Stella, to whom he had given his heart, was saying.

She was telling him all too clearly that she did not love him as he wanted desperately to be loved.

Because he was silent, Stella kissed his cheek.

"We will have a lovely time together and you must come to dinner tonight, David. The Devonshires are giving a ball and I know they will be delighted for you to join us. We are having a dinner party here first."

Slowly David took his arm away from her.

"I thought when we were in Simla together that you really loved me. I fell in love with you, Stella, but I knew it would be difficult for me to take a wife."

"Of course, it would be difficult," she agreed before he could say any more. "And it would be difficult now, but that need not stop us being together and being happy as we have been before."

She drew in her breath.

"I do love you, David. I love dancing with you and I love you kissing me, but I really could not face being an Army wife in a potty little house with very few servants."

"Would it matter if we loved each other?"

The question came from deep inside his heart and he asked it without really meaning to.

Stella gave a little laugh.

"I am afraid it would, and I am sure you would find it boring if I was not able to give parties for our friends and had to count every penny before we bought a saucepan, let alone a new dress."

She was laughing as she spoke and then she threw out her arms.

"Why worry about marriage? We can be together without it."

She was about to kiss David again when a servant opened the door.

"Major Watson to see you, Lady Sahib."

Stella moved quickly from David's side.

"I am afraid I am rather early," Major Watson said as he crossed the room. "But it was too dashed hot to stay outside and wait for the right moment to appear."

"I am so delighted to see you, Major, and of course you know Captain Ingle."

David had always thought that Major Watson was a self-opinionated and tiresome man, who did very little in the Army except ingratiate himself with the wives of his superior Officers.

He was, however, invariably invited to every Social function that took place in Calcutta.

He was notorious as a flirt and a failure as a soldier and David, like most of his contemporaries, had no use for him.

"I am afraid," he now addressed Stella, "I have to say goodbye. As it happens I am leaving for England this evening, so we will not be meeting for some time."

Stella gave a cry of dismay.

"Leaving for England? But why? How can you be going away again so quickly?"

"I think it all amounts to my business and that is something which is very difficult for any of us to avoid."

As David spoke he looked rather pointedly at Major Watson.

"If you were to ask me," said the Major, "business is usually an excuse for making one do something one does not want to do, so I avoid it whenever possible!"

"I am well aware of that," answered David, "and of course you are very clever."

There was a sarcastic note in his voice and yet he was certain that the Major was too conceited to notice it.

He walked to the door and Stella gave another cry.

"Oh, David, you cannot possibly go away tonight! I must see you."

"I am sorry, Stella, it is goodbye, perhaps for a long time."

"But surely you know when you are coming back?"

"I am not certain at the moment."

David reached the door and pulled it open as Stella caught hold of his arm.

"I want you to dine with us tonight," she breathed.

"It is very kind of you to ask me, but I am afraid it is impossible. *Goodbye,* Stella."

He moved away before she could stop him and as he ran down the stairs, he heard her call after him, but he did not look back.

As he walked out of the house, he felt he had learnt a lesson he would always remember.

It was that women like Stella were not looking for love, but for money and importance.

He was feeling so furious with himself that he had been deceived into believing that she really loved him.

He had been certain that if it was possible and he asked her to marry him she would accept.

'I was a fool to even think of it,' he told himself.

Then he knew as he went back to his barracks that

the Viceroy was right – the sooner he departed from India and was free of the Russians and Stella the better.

They both had one thing in common – one could *not* trust either of them.

Back at the barracks he ordered his batman to pack up everything he possessed.

"You going home, Sahib?" the batman asked.

"I am afraid so, Ali, and thank you very much for looking after me for so long."

"I miss you, Sahib. You very kind to me and I do hope you not away too long."

"If I do come back, I will ask for you at once, but it is not very likely."

He then went to see his Colonel and he found that he was expecting him. He had already guessed from what the Viceroy had told him that David would have to leave.

"I will miss you, Ingle," he said, "more than I can possibly say. But I am sure it is wise for you to be away from India at least for some time."

"That is just what His Excellency said to me, but you must know, Colonel, I have no wish to leave and I will miss the Regiment enormously"

"What you are really saying is that you will miss the very valuable work you have done in *The Great Game*. I know I need not tell you to be very discreet about what you say in England, however influential they may be."

David nodded.

"It is such an exciting story, Ingle, that it would be almost impossible for them to keep it from their wives and their friends. You know, as I do, that one unfortunate word could mean the end of a man's life."

"My lips are sealed after tonight, Colonel."

"I must, of course, congratulate you on coming into your grandfather's title," the Colonel continued. "But I am afraid it will mean the end of your Army career."

"That is what I am afraid of too," replied David. "I have the uncomfortable feeling there will be much for me to do when I reach home."

The Colonel was silent for a moment, then added,

"I have never had an Officer under me with such excellent prospects as yours. It is not only your work in *The Great Game* that has been outstanding, but also your good influence in the Regiment has helped me greatly. I can only say that I will miss you every day you are gone."

David was deeply touched.

"That is very kind of you, Colonel, and I know how much I will miss the men I have enjoyed training and my brother Officers have been extremely kind to me."

"I suppose it is *Fate* and when Fate takes a hand in our lives there is nothing we can do about it."

David decided that he must be right.

*

Later that night as the Steamship moved out of port, he stood on deck.

He watched the lights of Calcutta until he could not see them any longer.

Then he knew with a deep sigh that a chapter of his life had closed.

It had encompassed so much that he found it hard to believe it was really at an end.

There had been the Regiment, the thrill of his first mission in *The Great Game*, when he had been very near to death at least half-a-dozen times and there had been his many encounters with India's enemies, at all of which he had triumphed, as in the last encounter at Fort Tibbee, he had always been overwhelmingly successful.

At least he could say that, if he had done nothing else, he had made British rule a little stronger than when he had first set foot on Indian soil.

His only failure was Stella.

He had believed, perhaps foolishly, that she really loved him and he had thought about her every night when he went to bed.

He had been determined that if he survived his last mission over the frontier and his fight for Fort Tibbee, he would ask her to be his wife.

Although she had not known about it at the time, he was today in very different circumstances.

But impulsively, because she looked so lovely and desirable, he had then asked her the all important question without any preliminaries.

She had refused him – but she would not have done if she had known that he had inherited an ancient title that anyone would be proud of.

That, David told himself, was something he did not need from the woman to whom he would give his heart.

He wanted love.

The real love that his mother had had for his father.

The real love that to him was something wonderful and sacred.

Then he thought that he was a fool.

He was asking too much.

All women, and he despised them for it, wanted not a man who laid his soul at their feet, but who could place a diamond tiara on their head.

And whose rank would make the servants and shop keepers address them respectfully.

David looked up at the moon.

'I was asking for far too much,' he told the moon cynically. 'It is something that will *never* happen to me.'

CHAPTER THREE

David had plenty of time to think about himself in the seventeen days it took the Steamer to reach England.

He had not thought much about his family for years simply because he had hated his grandfather, the Marquis, and had more interesting issues to think about in India.

But now when he looked back, he remembered that his grandfather had been the eighth Marquis of Inglestone.

The Marquisate went back to the twelfth century.

His grandfather had married a daughter of the Duke of Dunstead and she had given herself as many airs as her husband did and they behaved, David thought, as if they were Royalty and expected everyone to bow to them.

His grandfather was little more than forty when his wife died, having borne him two sons and not surprisingly, he soon married again.

Lady Elizabeth Falcon was very different from his first wife. She enjoyed her life, was very intelligent and an excellent rider.

She had been married before but without children and made the Marquis a little more human. She was one of those people who made friends easily and thus she never found herself lonely.

They had not been married for a year when a son, Richard, was born and he took after his mother, not only in looks, as he was a handsome lad.

When he went to Eton, he became Head of School and Captain of Cricket and later at Oxford he took a First.

The Marquis, although he did not often say so, was proud of his son and was determined that he should make a good marriage.

After Oxford Richard went abroad for a short time and came back thrilled with his time in France and Spain.

It was then his father had said to him,

"I have arranged for your marriage – "

Richard had stared at him in astonishment.

"My marriage!" he exclaimed.

"I wish you to marry the daughter of the Duke of Sheldon, and her father is delighted to be united with our family."

"If I marry anyone," Richard had stated firmly, "I will marry someone I love and who loves me. I would not think of making an arranged marriage."

"You will do as you are told," his father told him sternly. "I will brook no nonsense from you, Richard, and I have already arranged for the Duke to bring his daughter to meet you and the rest of the family next week."

Richard did not reply, as he knew of old that it was hopeless and a great mistake to argue with his father. He had done so when he was young and had been overruled.

Two days before the Duke had arrived at Ingle Hall with his daughter, Richard left home and disappeared.

The Marquis was furious at his behaviour, but there was nothing he could do.

When, a few months later, he received a letter from his son, he almost had a stroke.

Richard informed him that he had married someone he was deeply in love with and who loved him.

"Her name," he had written, *"is Elizabeth Anson. Her father, who you will never have heard about, is a most distinguished scientist who has travelled all over the world and written several books on his discoveries.*

We are blissfully happy and I do hope that you will welcome Elizabeth when I bring her home."

The letter was written from Spain.

It was not until several weeks later that the Marquis had learnt that his son was in London and that he was able to communicate with him.

He then informed Richard that he had disobeyed his orders and behaved in a scandalous fashion. In addition he had then cut him off without a penny and he was no longer welcome at Ingle Hall.

The letter had not troubled Richard at all as he was madly in love with his wife and she worshipped him.

Their love was to increase over the years and when David was born, he merely added to their happiness.

David had a somewhat strange upbringing that was bizarrely different from his father's.

Richard had not been especially upset at being cut off without a penny, as he had money of his own.

His Godfather, who had been a very distinguished Statesman, had left him quite a considerable sum and this had grown while Richard was at Eton and Oxford as he had no need to spend any of it.

Now it paid for him, his wife and their small son to travel, as he always wanted to do, around the world.

David therefore had the strangest education any boy could possibly experience.

He had nurses who spoke to him in Arabic and he learnt Copt from some Egyptians who were friends of his father. He became virtually word perfect in ancient and modern Greek when they had lived in Greece for quite a considerable time.

Apart from this, Richard, with his own excellent if conventional education, enjoyed teaching his son all he had learnt himself.

They were blissfully happy, as three people seldom are happy, as they travelled from country to country and Richard always felt that there was somewhere in the world he had not yet explored.

David was nearly twenty-one when disaster struck.

When they were in North Africa, his father caught a fever which was known to have no cure.

It was lethal in his case and he died in three days.

His wife and son both found it hard to believe that anything so terrible could happen so quickly.

He was buried in a small cemetery by the British Embassy and the Ambassador arranged for the widow and her son to return to England.

David's mother was so prostrate with misery that he had to arrange everything.

What worried him was that his father had left very little money, so that by the time the funeral was paid for and the lodgings where they had been staying, he only had just enough for their travelling expenses.

Because they had then no home in England, he had thought that the only thing he could possibly do was to go to the family house in Kent, Ingle Hall.

He had never been there himself, but his father had often told him how magnificent it was, having been built in Elizabethan times.

Every generation had contributed to the collection of pictures, furniture, china and silver and, having been strictly entailed from one generation to the next, it had just grown and grown.

Ingle Hall was now one of the treasures of England.

As he had never seen it, it was difficult for David to realise not only its beauty but its significance and because his father had been exiled, he always expected to be exiled himself.

But since his mother was, in addition to her grief, in poor health, he decided to take her to the family home until they could find a home of their own.

The Ambassador had very kindly sent a cable to the Marquis, informing him of David and Lady Richard Ingle's imminent arrival.

When their ship reached the white cliffs of Dover, David thought that this was another land of discovery for him, like those he had enjoyed with his father.

They had a particularly tiring journey, ending in a post chaise before they finally reached Ingle Hall.

It was past six o'clock in the evening and David's mother was completely exhausted.

"I am sorry, darling, to be such a nuisance," she had murmured earlier in the day.

"You are nothing of the sort, Mama, and as soon as we reach Ingle Hall, you must go to bed at once and stay there until you feel better."

She had smiled at David and put up her hands to touch his cheek.

"You have been so kind and wonderful to me and I know that your father would be very grateful."

Tears came into her eyes when she spoke about her dear husband and her son bent down and kissed her.

"You have been so very brave, Mama, and we must only hope that Grandpapa will be pleased to see us."

He knew as he spoke that his mother was thinking that this was most unlikely.

He had not told her that at present their situation was desperate as he only had a few coins left and he hoped that when he contacted his father's Bank he would find that matters were not as bad as they seemed.

But he was mature enough to realise that they had spent a great deal of money recently on their journeys.

His father had once or twice said that if things grew worse then both of them would have to seek out some way of earning money.

David had thought at the time that it would not be so difficult as there was no one as clever as his father and he was sure that he could put his many languages to use.

Actually neither he nor his mother had ever thought about money very seriously – it had always been left in his father's hands.

They arrived at Ingle Hall and as they drove up the drive, David was most impressed by the huge ornamental gold-tipped gates.

At his first sight of the house, he realised that his father had not exaggerated in his description of it.

It was very large and impressive with its mellowed red bricks and fascinating Elizabethan chimneys and it was almost breathtaking in the sunshine.

The post chaise drew up outside the front door and two footmen ran a red carpet down the steps.

David helped his mother out carefully and she was, he realised, almost on the verge of collapse, but with her usual bravery, she raised her head and walked up the steps on his arm.

A formidable butler with white hair addressed her,

"Welcome and we were expecting you, my Lady, and his Lordship's waiting for you and Mr. David in his study."

David smiled at him.

"You must be Newman. My father often spoke of you and how kind you were when he was a little boy."

Newman looked delighted.

"All of us loved Lord Richard," he said, "although he be a real pickle from the time he were born!"

David laughed.

"I can well believe it."

Slowly because it was impossible for his mother to move quickly, they both followed Newman down a high-ceilinged corridor.

He stopped at a door and opened it to announce,

"Lady Richard Ingle, my Lord, and Mr. David."

David realised that he was in the enchanting study his father had often described to him.

There were books in inlaid marquetry cabinets and pictures that would be the envy of every art collector.

From a Regency writing table glittering with a gold inkpot, the Marquis rose.

It was the first time that David had ever seen his grandfather and he was not as imposing nor as autocratic-looking as he had expected.

What had happened was that he had indeed shrunk with the years and now aged eighty-seven, he was not the domineering figure he had been in earlier days.

Yet when he spoke, his voice was still sharp, hard and aggressive,

"So you have come home after all these years – "

David could not shake his hand, because his mother was supporting herself on his right arm.

"As you will have heard, Grandpapa, my father has died of an Eastern fever and after we had buried him I have brought my mother back to England."

"So I can see, but that is no concern of mine!"

The way he spoke was so obviously unpleasant that David's mother gave a little exclamation.

David moved her to a chair and helped her sit down and then he walked a few paces nearer to his grandfather.

"I think you can see, Grandpapa, that my mother is not in good health and the shock of losing my father has almost been too much for her. I know we have a great deal to say to each other, but I would be exceedingly grateful if you would allow her to rest and then it would be best if she could see a doctor."

For a moment the Marquis did not reply, and then he muttered,

"Where your mother rests or does not rest is not my problem. Your father married her against my will, and I, therefore, do not consider her or you to be any part of my family."

David stared at him in astonishment and then with an effort, he enquired,

"Are you turning us away?"

"I am making it clear to you that your father chose to ignore what I had arranged for him. I communicated to him very clearly at the time that I no longer thought of him as my son and he would have no claim upon me at all."

Remembering that he had hardly any money, David was for the moment shocked into silence and then he tried in a conciliatory tone,

"I can easily understand, Grandpapa, that you were annoyed with my father. Equally that was over twenty-two years ago. He is now dead and he always spoke to me with great affection for this house and his brothers."

"Your father chose his own life and I see no reason, now he is dead, that I should accept either his wife whom I despise, nor you, her son."

"I would very much hope, Grandpapa, that we can talk this over sensibly and perhaps a little more amicably tomorrow morning. As I have just requested, I think it is essential for my mother to rest after the long journey."

"I told the servants to keep whatever conveyance you came in, and it is waiting for you at the front door!"

David drew in his breath.

"Are you really turning us away with my mother so sick and on the point of collapse, as you can well see?"

"That is not my concern," the Marquis replied, "and the sooner you both leave this house, where you are not at all welcome, the better I shall be pleased."

As he spoke he sat down at his writing desk as if to carry on with what he was doing when they came in.

For a moment David was at a loss for words.

He was also thinking that he might not have enough money to pay for the post chaise let alone lodgings for the night.

It passed through his mind that he would have to crawl to his grandfather for help and then pride told him it was a course he should not take.

He merely turned round and walked to the chair his mother was sitting on and gently he drew her to her feet.

"I am very sorry, Mama, but I am afraid we have to journey a little further."

She looked towards the Marquis.

"Whatever you may say or think about me, David is your grandson and I am very shocked that you should treat him in this fashion."

The Marquis raised his head.

"As I have said, your husband disobeyed me and I have no use for either his wife or his offspring."

The way he spoke was hurting and offensive.

David knew that nothing more could be gained and so he merely drew his mother towards the door.

And he was not surprised to find that Newman was waiting outside.

Between them they carried his mother back through the hall, down the steps and into the post chaise.

It was only then that David spoke,

"Tell me, Newman, where we can go. I cannot take my mother far. You can see how exhausted she is."

"I knows, Mr. David, and it's real sorry I am for her Ladyship and you."

"Is there a hotel or a lodging house near here?"

Newman shook his head.

"I thinks you'd best go to the Vicar. He's a kindly man. He'll never refuse anyone and he were always very fond of your father."

David smiled at him.

"Thank you, Newman, I am most grateful to you."

The Vicar had then accepted them and understood immediately what had happened at Ingle Hall.

"Your grandfather is a hard man," he said, "and he never forgave your father for refusing to be married to the distinguished lady he had chosen for him."

"It was a decision my father never regretted."

"I can understand that no one wants his wife chosen for him by someone else and I am glad that your father was so happy."

"Divinely happy – and my mother is finding it very difficult to be without him."

He carried her upstairs and with the gentle help of the Vicar's servant, a nice woman from the village, they undressed her and got her into bed.

It was only when David went to say goodnight to her that he realised how seriously ill she was.

It was essential that she should see a doctor and it was arranged by the Vicar that one would call on the next morning.

But it was too late.

Elizabeth passed away peacefully in her sleep.

David was certain that she had joined his father and they were together again.

He knew that if he was honest, it would have been virtually impossible for her to make a new life in England without her husband and, as he knew, without any money.

The first task that he must undertake even before his mother was buried was to pay a visit his father's Bank and talk to the Manager.

He was told in no uncertain terms and there was no arguing about it, that there was no money – what had been deposited originally by Lord Richard's Godfather had been gradually drained away.

The Bank had informed Lord Richard several times that there was very little left.

"When I sent your father the last hundred pounds," the Manager said, "I told him there was no more money. I also, on his instructions, sold the few treasures he still owned."

David had then gone back to the Vicarage with just enough to give the Vicar what he owed him for paying the post chaise and for his mother's burial.

He had obtained this sum by selling the delightful silver engagement ring his father had given his mother as well as the pearl necklace he had bought for her when they had first visited India.

They had only been in India a short time and David had been twelve at the time, yet he had always remembered the beauty of the country, which had excited him more than any other country his father had taken him to.

He knew then what he wanted to do.

He travelled to London to call on the Secretary of State for India, Lord Clare, who as it happened, had known his father and had been extremely interested in the different places in the world where Lord Richard and his wife turned up unexpectedly.

When David told him of his father's death and that of his mother, he was most sympathetic.

"I have asked to come and see you, my Lord, as I want more than anything else to join a Regiment in India."

Lord Clare had been delighted.

"We are very short of Officers in the Cavalry – "

Then he hesitated before he added,

"As you have this affection for India and as you are your father's son, I cannot help thinking that you could be of tremendous help to the Viceroy in one particular way in which we are attempting to better the Russians."

David's eyes lit up.

"Are you talking of *The Great Game*, my Lord?"

"You have heard of it?" Lord Clare exclaimed.

"My father told me about it," David replied, "and if there is one thing I would wish to do more than anything else it is to take part in what seems to me the most exciting and original 'game' that has ever been invented!"

"You are quite right about that, but I am sure your father told you of its dangers, its difficulties and the fact that you take your life in your own hands every day."

"It is exactly what I want to do, my Lord."

His enthusiasm pleased Lord Clare, who had indeed been extremely fond of Lord Richard.

David sailed out to India with a letter to the Colonel of his Regiment and also a private one to the Viceroy.

David had been deeply shocked at losing both his father and his mother and the prospects ahead of him took his mind off himself.

Occasionally, he thought it was really rather sad to have no relatives and no family and to be, to all intents and purposes, entirely on his own.

When he thought of his grandfather and the way he had behaved, he had wanted to forget that he was an Ingle, just as his father had done when he made his life in his own way.

*

Yet now at the age of ninety-two, his grandfather was dead and, although it seemed incredible, were both his sons by his first marriage.

As David ruminated through the whole scenario, he could not help knowing that his father would have laughed.

After he had completely broken all his ties with his family, his son was now the ninth Marquis of Inglestone.

If this had happened to his father, he could have looked forward to a long life as the Head of the family and as the owner of Ingle Hall and two thousand acres of good Kentish land.

As the ship drew nearer to English shores, he was hoping that the rest of the family, if any existed, would not resent him or feel that he was an usurper.

At the same time he could not believe that they had much love for his grandfather and maybe a number of them hated him as much as he did.

Even now he could again feel his fury as he assisted his mother from the study and carried her with Newman's help into the post chaise.

He wondered if the Vicar was still at the Vicarage – he had meant to write to him from India, but had been too preoccupied to write to anyone.

He could not help recognising that coming back to England after so long, he had in fact no friends there at all. His father was always meeting his Eton or Oxford friends in strange and unexpected places.

"Fancy meeting you here!" they would say to him almost before Lord Richard could greet them.

'My friends,' David mused, 'are scattered all over the world in strange places. I have to think of England as a foreign country I have not explored before.'

Equally as he drove from London to Ingle Hall, he felt apprehensive.

Maybe there were many family members there who would resent his taking over his grandfather's place – they would remember all too clearly how his father had run off and married someone they had not approved of.

It was five o'clock in the afternoon when the post chaise turned in at the gates and he well remembered being impressed by them when he had first come to Ingle Hall with his dear mother.

Now, when he regarded the lodges, they looked, he thought, as if no one was living in them.

The post chaise ambled on and once again he was entranced by the beauty of the Elizabethan house.

Only as they drove into the courtyard was he aware that the house looked very different from five years ago.

The mullion windows needed cleaning, the flower-beds along the front of the house were filled with weeds.

There was certainly no red carpet being run down the steps before the front door.

David had deliberately not telegraphed through the time or day of his arrival as he was not at all certain when it would be.

Also he had no idea who might be in the house.

He presumed there would be servants, although it was doubtful if Newman would still be there as butler.

He therefore paid the driver of the post chaise, but asked him to wait just in case the house was closed up.

'I may have to go somewhere else to find the key,' he told himself, but he thought it a little unlikely.

Although his grandfather had been dead for some time, the Solicitors, if no one else, would appreciate that he must come to Ingle Hall at some time.

He reached the front door and raised the knocker – he had looked for a bell but there did not appear to be one.

Then, as he was just wondering what he should do, there was the sound of footsteps.

The door creaked open slowly.

To his astonishment he found himself facing a very pretty young girl with long golden hair and blue eyes.

She stared at him for a moment and then exclaimed,

"Oh, it is *you*! I thought it might be and I am sorry I have kept you waiting."

David followed her into the hall which was just as he remembered it, except he could see it was very dusty – the ashes of what had once been a fire were lying untidily in the great medieval fireplace.

"I am sorry," David began, "I did not give anyone

notice of my intended arrival, as I was not certain when it would be."

"We waited and waited," replied the girl, "but the Solicitors told us that there was no reply to the cable they had sent to India."

David smiled.

"Well, I am here now, and as you know who I am, perhaps you will be kind enough to introduce yourself."

"I am Benina Falcon, my Lord, and I am a distant relative of your father's mother."

David put out his hand.

"I am delighted to meet you, Benina."

"I am afraid you will find it rather uncomfortable, but it has been so impossible for Nanny and me to do very much to the house, although we *have* tried."

David did not understand her, but for the moment he did not ask questions.

He merely answered,

"As I have come down from London, I hope there is something for dinner and I would now love a cup of tea."

Benina laughed and he thought it a most attractive sound.

"Nanny and I did not think you might like tea, but I will run and tell her and will bring it to you in the study. We have been using that room because it is cosier than the others. I expect you know the way."

She was gone before David could reply.

He stared after her, feeling somehow bewildered.

'Surely there must be some servants in the house,' he thought.

Although Newman has probably retired by now, he must have been replaced and David remembered that when he was last here, there had been two footmen in the hall.

It all seemed so weird.

He walked down the corridor to the room where he had met his grandfather and, as he did so, he noticed again how dusty everything was.

'Surely even though my grandfather is now dead, the servants could at least dust the furniture.'

He walked into the study and it was much cleaner.

There were flowers arranged in two large bowls by the window, and the fire, although it was not needed, had been properly laid.

He recalled his grandfather standing at the writing desk and speaking to him in a most offensive manner and he had then been turned out of this house, and told he was no longer a member of the family and yet now he was here taking his grandfather's place.

He gave a little sigh, feeling that it was not going to be easy. If only his beloved father had lived, how different everything would have been.

It was twenty minutes before Benina came hurrying back with his tea on a tray and put it down by the sofa.

"I am afraid Nanny has only been able to make you a very small sandwich," she announced, "but we have run out of bread. She also says she has no idea what she can give you for dinner tonight."

David walked towards the sofa and sat down.

"Suppose you pour out my tea and at the same time tell me what is going on. I had rather hoped Newman was still here, but I suppose he has retired or is he dead?"

"Newman had to go to the workhouse – "

"The *workhouse!* What do you mean?"

"The Marquis refused either to pay or feed him!"

David stared at her as if he could not believe what he had just heard.

"I am afraid you are going to be very shocked when you learn what has been happening here," added Benina. "But as the servants were given no wages, they left one by one. Then, as the Marquis refused to feed those who were left, who were all old like Newman, they were forced to go to the workhouse."

David put his hand up to his head.

"I find this quite impossible to believe. Why was there no money? Why could the servants not be paid?"

"I think there *was* some money," replied Benina, "but your grandfather would not spend it."

She gave a little sigh and sat down on an armchair.

"To be honest, I think the Marquis became a little mad after he was eighty-nine. My mother and I came here the next year and he tried not to have us, but we told him we had nowhere to go, and finally, reluctantly, he gave in."

"I don't understand. You say you are a relative of my grandmother, but why did you come to live here?"

"It's a long story. My father did not get on with the rest of the Falcon family because, just like your father, he had married someone they all disapproved of."

David smiled.

"I know only too well how disagreeable relatives can be!"

"They were quite horrible to Papa and Mama and of course as we were only minor relations they paid very little attention to us – "

She gave a deep sigh, then continued,

"Except for your Grandmama who was always very kind and continually wrote to my father right up to the time of his death."

"So your father is dead," remarked David, trying to put the whole scenario into perspective.

"Yes, and so is my Mama," said Benina with a sob in her voice. "When Papa died, Mama came here, hoping that the Marchioness would be kind to her."

"And was she?"

"She tried to be, but I think the Marquis thought we were a tiresome expense and said that Mama and I would have to leave."

"But apparently you did not do so?"

"No, because the Marchioness died, and as we kept very quiet and lived in a different part of the house, I don't think the Marquis knew for some time that we were here."

"Then what happened?"

"He became very odd and was quite certain that he must save his money and not spend any of it."

"That does seem rather peculiar."

"It was terrible," Benina carried on. "He dismissed a great number of the staff, especially those who worked in the garden and the farm. Then he started on the household, who either left or clung on like Newman until they had to go because there was no food for them."

"And what happened to you?" enquired David.

Benina put her hand up to her face.

"It was terrible, absolutely terrible. My Mama was growing weaker and weaker, but we had nothing at all and nowhere to go."

"So what did you do?"

"Finally Mama cleverly persuaded the Marquis that he could save money on us because we would become his servants without payment. All he had to do was to feed us and we would clean what we could of the house and cook his meals."

David found this all very hard to believe.

How could any man, most especially a Marquis of Inglestone, behave in such an appalling manner?

"What we next did was to hide Nanny. We knew we could not do without her, and she had nowhere to go if she left us. She was kept out of sight, and the Marquis, as he was growing blind as well as everything else, believed that only Mama and I were in the house."

"It sounds incredible to me," sighed David.

"Everything about it was horrible, especially when Mama became really ill and we dared not send for a doctor at first as we knew that the Marquis would not pay for him. Finally, Nanny insisted I go and see the doctor and beg him on my knees to come even though he would not be paid."

"And did he come?"

"Yes of course he did and it was silly of us not to have asked him before."

There was silence for a moment, then she added,

"It was too late and Mama died. I think her heart was weak and because of having so little food, she had not the strength that she required to keep alive."

Benina's voice broke on the last words and David said quickly,

"I am sorry, desperately sorry to hear all this. But I still cannot appreciate why it should have happened."

"I cannot understand it either. Neither of us could believe that the Marquis had no money. I think in a mad way he thought he must keep it safe and not spend it."

"I will go and see the Bank Manager tomorrow," David told her. "Is there any sort of conveyance left in the stables or on the estate?"

"There are two horses, but they are put out to grass as the Marquis would not buy any food for them."

She gave a little sob before she continued,

"There were two others which died last winter, but I ride these two when I have the time."

"Until your grandfather died he kept Nanny and me running about all day fetching things for him and putting things back, mostly for no reason."

She paused and then explained,

"By this time he was so blind and thought Nanny was Mama and was quite content to let her dress him."

"But surely some of the family who came here must have known what was happening?"

"Lord Cecil had been killed in the Sudan with his Regiment. The Viscount spent most of his time in London and when he did come home, he was so uncomfortable and complained to Nanny and me about everything."

"I am not surprised!"

"When he knew that the Viscount was coming, the Marquis used to give us some money, just enough to buy food for the meals when he was in the house."

Her voice dropped to a whisper, as she added,

"Sometimes if we were clever, we would get a little more and keep it until after he had gone. But he did not come very often."

"Why did you not ask him for money?"

"I did do," answered Benina, "but the Viscount felt that his father had plenty of money, and if he did not want to spend it that was his business. Then he went back to London and did not return for a very long time."

David thought he could not blame him, so he said,

"What I have to do is to find out exactly what has happened to all the money. In the meantime I have some with me and I suggest, as your Nanny is doing the cooking, she will know how to spend it."

Benina gave a little jump for joy.

"If dear Nanny had not been clever enough to make the boys in the village snare some rabbits for us, I think we would have died from starvation!

"Luckily I had one or two small pieces of jewellery belonging to my mother that I managed to pawn."

She gave a little smile.

"Occasionally the Marquis would forget that he had given us money one day and gave us some more the next, saying it had to last for the week."

"I have never heard of anything quite so dreadful," exclaimed David. "And now you have to help me, unless, of course, you want to leave."

Benina's eyes opened very wide and then she asked in a hesitating voice,

"You are not – sending Nanny – and me away?"

"Not if you wish to stay, but I think people might think it strange that you are staying at Ingle Hall without a chaperone, even though we are vaguely related."

"Actually I think I must be your cousin two or three times removed."

David laughed.

"I suppose that should be close enough to make it respectable!"

"We do have Nanny as a chaperone," she asserted, almost aggressively.

"I hardly that think Nanny will be sufficient if we entertain our relatives or people who might call on me out of curiosity," countered David.

Benina did not reply and he added jokingly,

"You can hardly expect Nanny to cook luncheon and then sit down at the same table with us."

"Nanny said just that when I told her you wanted dinner, but I don't want you to see the dining room, as I have not had time to polish the candlesticks and the rest of the silver to make it look as you would expect it."

David chuckled.

"I think tonight we had best eat in the kitchen, but I shall be upset if there is nothing to eat, so please go and give Nanny this."

He took a five pound note from his pocket and then handed it to Benina.

She took it from him and stared at it.

"Nanny will think that she's dreaming! Have you any more like this one, my Lord?"

David chuckled again.

"I am a soldier so I am not rich, but I have enough money to prevent us from being hungry and I want to find out as fast as I possibly can, what on earth has happened to all my grandfather's money."

He was thinking that the Marquis had always been spoken of as a very rich man and he remembered his father telling him how he had often given large parties.

There had been a lavish ball for the Viscount on his twenty-first birthday besides fireworks in the park, and the house had been filled with guests and an army of servants to wait on them.

It just seemed so extraordinary that his grandfather had stopped cultivating the land and presumably had then driven out the farmers.

From what his father had told him, there had been a great deal of wealth amassed over the centuries and it had made the eighth Marquis of Inglestone a very rich man.

'I don't understand all this,' pondered David.

But it was a problem he had to solve and the sooner the better.

CHAPTER FOUR

Dinner was rather late.

Benina insisted on bringing it into the study where they were more comfortable.

She made David chuckle by telling him how Nanny had thought that the five pound note note he had given her must be fake.

At first she had laughed and put it on the table.

"Then what happened?" asked David.

Benina hesitated before replying,

"It was kept a secret from the Marquis, but I would suppose it's all right to tell you, my Lord?"

"Tell me what?"

"Well, one of the gardeners who had been here for years was instructed to leave and your grandfather thought that he had given up his cottage. But he managed to find work in the village and therefore never left it."

She threw up her hands.

"Of course, we were most grateful to him because he occasionally brought us vegetables when it was too cold for me to dig them up in the kitchen garden."

She paused to see if David was still interested.

"We were very grateful to him," she added quickly, "and his son has helped us move things when they were too heavy for Nanny and me."

"What you are saying," David smiled, "is that the son, whoever he is, went to buy the food for my dinner."

Benina clapped her hands.

"You are so clever and you are quite right! Nanny will be very upset if you don't enjoy it."

Actually it was tender meat, very well cooked and David did enjoy it.

He noticed that Benina was eating slowly as if her every mouthful was ambrosia from the Gods and she did look very thin.

He thought the same when he met Nanny and was certain that the lines on her face were owing to deprivation rather than age.

After the excellent meat, there was some fruit and following that cheese.

"We have not seen one of these for years," Benina enthused, "and my parents loved really good cheese."

David noticed that although she was delighted with the cheese, she could not eat very much.

Having been so long in India, he knew the reason only too well – people who had been starving could never eat very much until they gradually acclimatised themselves to more food.

They retired to bed early because he was tired.

David had found out from Benina that there was a chaise available for hire if he wanted it.

"What about our own horses?" he asked her.

"I think that they are too weak if you are going into town. They have been out to grass all winter and are only now getting enough to eat."

David's lips tightened.

If there was one thing that infuriated him most, it

was unnecessary cruelty to animals and he knew only too well what effect this would have on well bred horses.

"I am going to give you a list, Benina, of items we need urgently, like feed for the horses, and something for us to drink. Perhaps you will go into the village whilst I am seeing my grandfather's Bank Manager."

"I thought that is what you would do. I know it is very stupid of me, but I did not think before how we could gain access to the cellar."

"Did my grandfather have nothing to drink?"

"He did sometimes, I think just when he felt ill, but he kept the keys of the rooms and cupboards to himself, so I have never been in the cellar."

"I can see we have a lot of exploring to do, Benina, but I must go and see the Bank Manager first, so that we know exactly where we stand."

Benina agreed to this plan of action and then she took David upstairs.

He washed in a room that had obviously not been cleaned or dusted for a long time, but after cooking dinner, Nanny had done the best she could to the Master bedroom.

Actually David did not really feel like sleeping in his grandfather's bed, but he knew it would upset Benina and Nanny as they had taken so much trouble for him.

It was certainly an imposing room and had been the Master Suite for many generations.

The huge four-poster bed was hung with curtains that had faded and were torn but were still colourful.

David bade Benina goodnight and then he asked as an afterthought,

"Where do you and Nanny sleep?"

There was a little pause before she answered,

"You may think it perhaps rather impertinent of us, but we were not very comfortable in the old Nursery where your grandfather had put us and there were so many flights of stairs for Nanny to climb – "

She paused before she added apologetically,

"It was when the Marquis was so ill and required a lot of attention that we both moved down to this floor."

"That was quite right. It would have been silly for you to do otherwise."

Benina smiled.

"You are so kind and understanding, my Lord. We were so frightened you would be like your grandfather and turn us out immediately."

"I have already told you, Benina, that I need your help. There is no one else to tell me the appalling things that have been happening here and somehow I have to put it all right."

Benina drew in her breath.

"Can you – really?"

"I will do my best."

"I think you are wonderful and I must go and tell Nanny at once."

She ran to the door then stopped to look back.

"Thank you for being *you*. Nanny and I will have breakfast ready for you in the study at eight-thirty."

She was gone again before David could reply.

He heard her running down the corridor.

He thought as he undressed that he had expected to find strange goings-on at Ingle Hall.

Yet he had never anticipated there would be a very beautiful young girl to help him.

'It is really lucky,' he said to himself, 'because if I

was here alone with no servants, I would not know where to begin.'

He climbed into the vast bed and as he had not been able to sleep very much last night worrying about what was awaiting him, he fell asleep at once.

*

He woke early because having been a soldier it was what he was used to.

When he went downstairs, he found Nanny dusting the study.

"Good morning, Nanny."

She turned round and smiled at him.

"I hope, my Lord, you've had a good night's sleep, and if you want the truth, it's the first night for months that I haven't lain awake a-worrying."

David laughed.

"I am glad, but we all still have a lot of worrying to do and the first thing, as you know, Nanny, as there are no secrets from you, is to find out if we have any money."

"It's what I've been saying to myself over and over. But just where's it all gone? His Lordship certainly didn't spend it on riotous living!"

"I am sure," smiled David, "and thank you for the delicious dinner last night. I want you to buy anything that you need from the village, so that I can with luck eat many more delicious meals!"

He saw Nanny was pleased at his praise.

"Do you think that the butcher and the baker and whoever else there is in the village will allow you to open an account or will they expect to be paid cash down?"

"I thinks when I a-tells them your Lordship's going to put things back to normal, they'll all be flying flags and singing in the streets."

Her voice changed as she added seriously,

"It's been really terrible these past years to see the cottagers a-needing their roofs thatched, the shops closing down because there weren't customers and the pensioners dying 'cos his Lordship wouldn't give them any money."

"Why did no one do anything about it, Nanny?"

"The Vicar did his level best, but when his Lordship threatened to reduce his stipend, he gave what he could out of his own pocket."

"I must try to pay him back for what he has spent," David said, as if he was speaking to himself. "But first I have to find out what has happened to all the money."

Benina sent the gardener's son to order a carriage to take him into Canterbury.

It arrived at ten o'clock and it was not the smartest vehicle and the horse was not very fast.

David knew that the first thing he wanted more than anything else was some decent horses to ride, but it was no use ruminating about what he required before he had the money to pay for it.

As he picked up his hat in the hall, Benina came running down the stairs and he knew she had been tidying his bedroom.

"Are you going now, my Lord?" she asked.

"The sooner I go, the sooner I will come back and then we will know where we are."

She stood still beside him for a moment and then she murmured,

"I am praying now as I prayed last night that you will find what you want and everything will turn out for the best."

"Thank you, Benina, and I think that we will need all your prayers to put matters straight."

He climbed into the carriage, wishing that he could drive himself.

He sat back on the upholstered seat and, as it was a sunny day, the hood was raised.

As they drove down the drive he could see first the dilapidated lodge – his grandfather must have sacked those who had lived there.

Then he was aware of the really pathetic condition of the village. Benina had not been exaggerating when she had told him that every cottage needed to be rethatched.

Both the gates were off their hinges and the gardens that David was sure used to be full of spring flowers were untended.

As he passed the Church, he saw there were bricks missing from the top of the tower and the gutters round the main building had fallen down.

He was thankful when they were out of the village and into the countryside, so that he could not see any more.

He had no idea how far the land belonging to Ingle Hall went, but the hedges had not been cut for years and the field were unploughed or sown with any crop.

By the time he reached Canterbury, he was feeling exceedingly apprehensive.

What would he learn from the Bank Manager?

*

As soon as he entered the Bank and explained who he was, he was taken immediately into the Bank Manager's office and an elderly man received him respectfully.

"My name is Morley, my Lord," he began, "and I was expecting that, as soon as you had arrived, you would honour us with a visit."

"I arrived last night, and having seen the condition of Ingle Hall, I am waiting for you to tell me exactly what the current situation is."

He sat down in a comfortable armchair which Mr. Morley held ready for him.

"I find it difficult, my Lord, to tell you how strange matters have been these last years."

"In what way, Mr. Morley?"

"His late Lordship was always exceedingly careful about money, and when he reached old age, I think, to be honest, it became an obsession with him."

"How?"

"I believe he thought that he would lose his money and that he could trust no one."

"So what did he do?"

"He started nearly four years ago to draw out from the Bank everything he possessed."

"*Everything*!" exclaimed David.

"He insisted on selling all his shares," Mr. Morley continued. "They were all in Companies paying out good dividends and were promising investments for the future."

"But surely his firm of Solicitors would have had said something about this to my family?"

"I don't think, my Lord, there were many of your family left with the exception, of course, of his Lordship's elder son, Viscount Stone, and his second son, Lord Cecil."

"Did they not say anything about it?"

"Lord Cecil was away from home for some years before he was killed in battle, and I think to be honest, the Viscount was far too intimidated by his father to question anything he did."

"Did no one else make any enquiries? There must have been some cousins or other relatives of the Ingles?"

"If there were, or there are, they did not contact me and I think the Marquis would not entertain any of them at

Ingle Hall. I was convinced that if they communicated with him, he would not answer."

David drew in a deep breath.

"Now please tell me exactly what has happened?"

"The late Marquis took out of the Bank practically everything he owned. I tried to expostulate with him, but he would not listen. He merely demanded that I sold share after share and he came and collected the proceeds himself every month – mostly in coinage."

David stared at the Bank Manager.

"Are you saying that my grandfather, old though he was, came here himself and carried every penny away."

"That is exactly what happened, my Lord, and, of course, we did not talk about him in the town or anywhere else in case he should be set on by highwaymen or robbers when he was driving back home.

"It always astonished me that, as his Lordship had very few servants to guard him, the robbers did not break into Ingle Hall and steal what he had secreted there."

David stared at him,

"Are you saying that my grandfather collected his money in cash that must have come to a considerable sum and then carted it all back to Ingle Hall?"

"That is exactly what occurred, my Lord, but what happened to it afterwards I have no idea."

For a moment David was speechless.

Then Mr. Morley continued his story,

"I have a complete list of what has been sold and what has been taken away and I obtained the highest price possible for the items we sold for him in the open market."

"I really cannot understand why he was doing this," murmured David.

"It is something I have asked myself thousands of times, my Lord, but I never found an answer."

"And what is left, Mr. Morley?"

He knew that this was the most important question.

"I am afraid, my Lord, you will be upset to know that the answer is in fact very little."

"I have always believed that my grandfather, when he came into the title, was an exceedingly rich man."

"He was, my Lord, and if the money he has taken from this Bank is still in existence, as it should be, then it is worth nearly two million pounds!"

David gasped.

He had realised that as the Head of the family, his grandfather was rich, but he had not thought he was as rich as that in actual cash.

And if one included the house, its contents and the estate, the total would amount to considerably more.

"I must tell you, my Lord," Mr. Morley carried on, "there were some shares which we could not sell but which may be worth a great deal more in the future than they are at present. I have a list of them."

He took a piece of paper from the table.

"Your grandfather, my Lord, invested in steamships when they were first driven by oil. However, he invested into an English Company that has not done as well as the Americans."

He handed the list to David.

"My directors believe it has prospects, although at the moment the dividends are hardly worth mentioning."

David looked down at the paper he was holding.

He saw that the Marquis had, as the Bank Manager said, quite a number of other investments.

America, he had been told, was booming and it was therefore reasonable to believe they might be worth a great deal more in the future.

"There are several shares, my Lord, in Companies that are involved in developing inventions for machinery and photography. But they are of little value at present, but we can hope that they will prove successful in the future."

"I think there could be every likelihood that they will, but equally I need a great deal of money now to put the estate in order."

"I have been told so, my Lord, and I can only hope that by some miracle you will be able to find the money your grandfather withdrew from us."

"Do you think that it could be hidden somewhere in Ingle Hall?" David asked him.

Mr. Morley held up his hands in a helpless gesture.

"How can we possibly tell? I think before he died his Lordship was not reasonable in any way, nor was he, I feel, entirely aware of what was happening around him."

David thought this was true, seeing the condition of the house and the grounds.

He then asked the Bank Manager if he could have an overdraft and some cash immediately.

"I have spent what I had when I left India on the journey and providing myself and the two people in Ingle Hall with something to eat last night. I have no wish to go hungry tonight or next week while I look round to see what has happened to the two million pounds that should still be safely in your keeping."

"I only hope that you will find it, my Lord, and of course, as we have been of service to the Inglestone family for many years, we will be pleased to permit your Lordship to overdraw a reasonable amount without security."

"As you are well aware, Mr. Morley, everything in Ingle Hall is entailed, yet I cannot help thinking that I will be able to find something I can either sell or pawn until we set matters straight or better still, find the enormous fortune my grandfather has hidden away."

"We are only too willing to help in every way we can, my Lord, but as you are well aware, I am responsible to our Head Office in London, who will undoubtedly ask questions if anything unusual occurs at this branch."

"I am most grateful to you and also for the way you have kept this unhappy affair secret. Please continue to do so, as I have no wish to have the newspapers hammering on my door or people coming to stare at Ingle Hall."

"They would have been far too frightened to do so when your grandfather was alive. I heard he threatened to shoot anyone who wandered round Ingle Hall at night!"

David had not heard of this, but made no comment.

Then he asked Mr. Morley for an advance of one hundred and fifty pounds for which he signed a cheque.

He shook him warmly by the hand and thanked him for his cooperation.

"As you can imagine, my Lord, it is to the Bank's advantage, as well as to yours, that the money is found."

"I promise you I will do my best, and without it, as you realise better than anyone else, life is going to be very difficult for me."

The Bank Manager smiled.

"I believe, just like your father, Lord Richard, that you will eventually win your way through."

David was amused.

His father had married who he wanted and gone off on his explorations and in consequence he became a hero in the eyes of his friends and those in Canterbury who were old enough to remember him.

As he drove back, he was trying to think out in his own mind what he should do first.

Actually there was no question about it – he had to find the hidden money.

He reasoned it out.

If his grandfather had gone mad in his old age and would not trust the Bank with his money, he would surely not have trusted anyone else.

Therefore it was quite obvious that the money was hidden somewhere in Ingle Hall or on the estate.

Such a large amount especially as it was in coinage, could not be pushed into the back of a drawer, nor could it be put in a small safe as it would take up too much space.

But there were enough rooms at Ingle Hall to hide a herd of elephants!

*

David returned to be greeted excitedly by Benina.

She ran down the steps as soon as the chaise came to a standstill.

He thought as he saw her approach how pretty she really was and he remembered that he had no time to think about anything except the task ahead of him.

He paid the driver and then walked into the house, recognising that Benina was longing to find out what had happened at the Bank.

She was controlled and tactful enough not to ask him anything until they had reached the study.

Then she regarded him questioningly with her large blue eyes and as he sat down, David told her quietly,

"I don't know whether it is worse or better than I had anticipated."

"What has happened? Please tell me," she pleaded. "I have been praying all the time you have been away."

"I am sure that your prayers helped me. The Bank Manager and I have reached the conclusion that it is quite impossible for the money, and it is indeed a large sum, to have been hidden anywhere but in this house."

"Here!" Benina exclaimed. "But where could the Marquis have concealed it?"

"That is what you and I have to find out. Although he was mad, he was very clever, as mad people often are, and it is not going to be easy."

"We must start looking at once, my Lord, otherwise there may not be anything for us to eat!"

David smiled.

"It is not as bad as that. I have arranged to have an overdraft. It is not a very large one, but we must at first be grateful for small mercies."

"I shall be grateful for anything as long as we don't have to be as hungry as we have been this last few months. It was terrible when Nanny began to feel ill and I thought I might be left entirely alone here."

"Nanny can now eat until she is as fat as she ought to be," said David, "and the same applies to you. You are far too thin and I have often been told that thin women are querulous and disagreeable!"

He was teasing, but Benina answered indignantly,

"I am *none* of those things."

"I know," smiled David, "but it is something I do not want you to become."

"Then let's start looking right away!"

"I think we would feel better if we had luncheon first, and I am certain that Nanny would be most annoyed if we let it get cold."

"You are quite right, my Lord, but may I go to the kitchen and tell her what you have told me?"

"Yes, of course, Benina, we are all in this adventure and if we fail, we will have no one to blame but ourselves."

"We are *not* going to fail," insisted Benina.

"Well, before we start our search, I intend to find a key to the cellar or break down the door!"

"Oh, I forgot to tell you, my Lord. How stupid of me! I was so excited to see you back that I forgot."

"What did you forget?"

"I found the key. It was hidden in a drawer in what is now your bedroom. Your grandfather put it right at the back behind a Bible and some old letters. I am sure that no one would have thought to look in there."

"Well done, Benina! If you have the key, let's go and explore the cellar. Perhaps we might find some wine down there."

He thought as he spoke, considering how mean his grandfather had been, it was most unlikely that there would be any at all.

However, to his joy there were a number of bottles of claret, brandy and wine that had been home-brewed.

The cellar was cavernous and with the lantern that Benina carried, it was easy to see it was practically empty.

There was nothing likely to be hidden in the bare walls or below the stony ground.

'After all,' David thought to himself, 'we are not looking for a few coins, but for a large amount of golden guineas.'

They could not be just shoved away in a corner.

When they emerged from the cellar, they found that Nanny was dishing up their luncheon.

"You're going to enjoy all this, my Lord," she said, "and so'll Miss Benina. I'm feeling more like myself again than I've felt for months."

"I have obtained some more money for you, Nanny, as soon as you need it, but there is one thing I want to do before we start chasing round the house and that is to get in touch with Newman."

"Oh, he's in the workhouse, my Lord."

"Yes, I know, Nanny, but is he in fairly good health and capable of coming back to help us?"

Nanny looked at David in surprise.

"That the best thing you've ever said, my Lord. If there's one person who knows every inch of the house, it's Mr. Newman and I knows that nothing'd please him more than being back here in what he has always considered his own home."

"As we are rather busy, Nanny, can you please get the gardener's son to go and tell him I am here and ask him when it will be convenient to pick him up."

"He will be thrilled!" exclaimed Benina.

"There must be someone in the village, who would be willing to drive him here if I pay him."

"I'll arrange it, my Lord," Nanny offered, "and I do knows that Mr. Newman'll be here as quick as he can, if he has to fly to do so!"

She picked up the roast lamb she had on a tray and carried it ahead of them into the study.

David found that Benina had laid the table they had used last night and when Nanny put down the lamb, all he had to do was to carve.

There were vegetables to go with it which he knew must have come from the garden, and David suspected that the gardener or his son were only too willing to help if they could be paid a few pennies for doing so.

David thought he must see the gardener and arrange for him to go to work in the garden again.

Yet he thought it would please Newman if he was the first to be working again at Ingle Hall.

He and Benina both enjoyed their luncheon and the bread-and-butter pudding Nanny had made for them with a little cream from the village was simply delicious.

"Have you had enough to eat, my Lord?" Benina asked when they had finished. "I expect Nanny forgot that you might like some cheese and biscuits."

"I have had plenty, Benina, and like you I want to get on with our task of searching the house. What I think is important now is to find all the keys. You have told me the safe was locked – "

"I will go and collect all the keys I can find."

"I will come with you, Benina, because I think we must do this in a systematic manner, starting at the bottom and working up until we reach the attics. If we cannot find the money, at least we will know what is in the house."

David paused for a moment and then he enquired,

"Is there an inventory of the contents anywhere?"

"Yes, it is in the library and I think, although I may be wrong, that your grandfather compiled it, hoping to find something he could sell and add to his pile of money."

David thought this unlikely as he was quite certain that his deranged grandfather was obsessed by the idea that everything Ingle Hall contained was his.

And he would resent anything, however small and unimportant, being stolen, mislaid or sold.

He might be wrong and yet if the old man had been so possessive to the point of hoarding all his money in his own hands, he would not have been willing to sell anything illegally.

It was, however, what David himself was prepared to do if he thought he could get away with it, but he knew the fuss there would be if anyone tried to evade the very strict laws of entailment.

Yet if there was anything that had been overlooked, he thought he would be absolutely justified in selling it and bring the land back into cultivation and restore the house to its former glory.

He and Benina set off as he had suggested.

Having investigated the wine cellar, they searched the other cellars and there was nothing except rubbish and an accumulation of dust and dirt from old age.

There was one cellar full of old boxes and trunks – they were all empty and had obviously been put there when the servants were too lazy to carry them up to the attics.

Their hands became filthy from handling them, but there was nothing to be found, not even old documents that might have been valuable.

He looked through the long inventory that Benina had managed to find of all the contents of the house, but he was not hopeful of finding anything that could be sold.

The exploration of the cellars took them the whole of the afternoon and into the evening.

When they came upstairs, Nanny made them wash their hands in the kitchen before, as she insisted, they went into the 'gentry' part of the house.

As they did so, David thought that he could hear someone arriving.

"I am sure there is a carriage outside," he remarked.

Nanny smiled at him.

"I expect it be the visitor you're expecting."

"Newman!"

He hurried from the kitchen into the front hall, but Benina beat him to the front door.

She opened it in time to see Newman stepping out of a farmer's cart.

He was looking, David thought, as he reached him, a great deal older with his white hair, but he was smiling broadly and was very obviously delighted to be back.

"I just didn't believe my old ears, Mr. David, when they tells me you had come home and wanted me."

"I want you very much, Newman, and I am so glad you are well enough to come."

"Well enough! There'll be nothing wrong with me, and I can see there's a great deal wrong with the house, but take it from me, his late Lordship, mad or not, was clever enough as a cartload of monkeys."

"He was lucky to get away with it all," commented David. "I would have thought that there would have been someone to stop him."

"If you would ask me, he was able to save himself by sacking everyone in the house and forcing Miss Benina and Nanny to do all the work."

"You may be right, Newman, but he must have put the money somewhere and we have to find it."

"And we'll find it, my Lord, but I'm not pretending to you or anyone else it's going to be easy."

When David retired to bed he thought this was true, yet somehow he felt rather more optimistic than he had felt before, now that Newman was back.

Of course, he told himself, he could bring in trained detectives to find what they were seeking, but that would be to make their problem public – sooner or later someone would be bound to talk.

He was certain if that did happen, it would evoke a great deal of sympathy, curiosity and greed.

As the prize was two million pounds, who would not be anxious to help in the search?

The more he thought about his situation, the more he was convinced that everything must be kept secret.

Newman, Nanny and Benina having been sworn to remain silent, the rest of the world would not be interested – they would think he was only trying to repair the damage wrought by neglect.

They would have no idea there were other reasons for their rampaging through the many rooms of Ingle Hall.

Already David was aware of the enormous amount of servants he would ultimately require to clean up the dirt and dust in every room.

He would need many expert craftsmen to repair the ceilings that had fallen down and put in new windowpanes.

But what was much more important than anything else was to find the money first.

As once again he went to bed in the four-poster in which his ancestors had slept, he sent up a little prayer to his father and mother as he felt that they more than anyone else would appreciate the enormous task in front of him.

A task that was not only essential for himself, but for the generations who would come after him.

CHAPTER FIVE

David came in late for breakfast and Benina looked at him questioningly.

Newman had already opened up the breakfast room and swept away most of the dust. It was a pretty room with long windows overlooking the garden and as it faced East, it received the first rays of the sun.

He had arranged their breakfast in the way it always had been in what he spoke of as 'the good old days'.

"I am sorry I am late," said David, as he entered.

"I wondered what had happened to you, my Lord," remarked Benina.

"I went to see Cosnet to tell him that he was to take over the garden."

Cosnet was the man he had been told had hidden himself away so that he could keep his cottage and his son had secretly helped Nanny and looked after the horses.

"What I have arranged," said David helping himself to eggs and bacon, "is that Cosnet will do what he can in the garden until I find him some more help. Ben, his son, will groom the horses and run messages."

Benina laughed.

"He will be kept busy."

"I thought you would say that, Benina, as I just sent him on one that will meet with your approval."

"What can that be?"

"I have told him to instruct the butcher to give the pensioners sufficient meat and sausages for three days and then to repeat the order until I tell him to stop."

Benina clapped her hands together.

"Oh, my Lord, only *you* could have done anything so wonderful. They will be so thrilled."

"I only hope they will be and I have also told Ben to tell the grocer to give them bread, butter and cheese. At least they will not starve."

For a moment Benina could not speak and then she exclaimed,

"I did not think anyone with your name could be so marvellous!"

"It is what I will have to be in the future, whether I like it or not. I just cannot have the Marquis of Inglestone going down in posterity as an evil monster!"

"That is just what I think your grandfather was."

"Now, what we must convene, as soon as we have finished breakfast, is a Council of War. So please will you tell Newman and Nanny to come to the study and you and I will be waiting for them there."

Benina gave a little laugh.

"Everything is becoming more and more exciting, I was beginning to think I was living in a backwater where nothing ever happened, except that Nanny and I grew older every minute."

"Now you have to be young again! And I think you are already making a good job of it."

David looked at her as he spoke.

With the sun shining through the windows onto her golden hair, she looked ethereally lovely.

At the same time he was aware that her blue dress was the same one she had worn the day before and the day before that – it was patched and darned in several places.

However, he told himself it was too soon to worry about clothes as, if their next exploration was as dirty as it had been yesterday, it was no use wearing anything decent.

David finished his second cup of coffee, then went off to the study.

He sat down, as his grandfather had, at the beautiful Regency writing desk and he could not help thinking that the desk and its gold inkpot would bring in a considerable amount if it was sold to a collector in London.

Then he told himself firmly it was not his to sell, but perhaps in their explorations in the next few days, they would find something which was not on the inventory.

Nanny and Newman entered the study and Nanny piped up,

"Now you're not to keep us for too long, my Lord, if you wants a good luncheon. I've got a chicken to pluck and that takes time!"

David smiled at her.

"I will not keep you long, Nanny. It is just that I want us four to know what we are doing and not waste any unnecessary time about it."

"If you're talking about a-finding all that money, it can't be found quick enough for my liking."

"I am doing my best, Nanny."

"Of course, he is," said Benina almost indignantly. "No one could have worked any harder than he and I did yesterday."

"And a nice mess you made of yourselves!"

David held up his hand.

"Now listen to me, all of you. First and foremost, everything we say in this room is a secret and known only to ourselves. We must be so very careful that, through an unwary word or talking too loudly when others are about, the outside world does not find out what we are doing."

He thought as he spoke how dangerous it had been in India when it was whispered what anyone in *The Great Game* was doing and in most cases it ended in the death of one of its members.

"We will be very careful," Benina agreed softly.

"Now what we have to do is to search everywhere, but not to waste time by going to the most unlikely places."

"That's good commonsense," remarked Nanny.

"What I want to ask you, Newman, is if you have any ideas where my grandfather might have concealed the money he brought back from the Bank?"

"I well remembers his Lordship going to the Bank," replied Newman, "on the first of every month, but I'd no idea what he was going for, although I hoped it were funds to pay our wages."

"When he came back, what did he do?"

"That's difficult for me to answer, my Lord, usually he went in the morning and came back before luncheon. I would be in the dining room getting things ready."

He saw that David looked disappointed and added quickly,

"There were footmen in the hall until his Lordship sacked them, but we can't get in touch with them now."

"Of course not, and even if we did, we would have to explain why we are so interested in what my grandfather was carrying."

Newman put his fingers up to his forehead.

"Now I thinks about it," he said, "I've an idea that I seen him once going up the stairs with a parcel in his arms.

I can't be certain what sort of parcel it were. I just thinks as how he's going up to his bedroom and I expects I says to him, 'luncheon'll be ready in five minutes, my Lord'."

David was listening intently.

"That does sound as if what he brought back from the Bank might be on the first floor."

"It seems sensible for him to hide it in his bedroom or somewhere near to him," suggested Benina.

"That's right," Nanny agreed. "If he was worrying about his precious money, he'd not want it to be out of his reach."

"Very well, that's just what I want to know. Now Miss Benina and I will start searching the first floor, and when Newman has time he can look at some of the rooms on the ground floor. This is going to take time."

"Of course it is," came in Benina, "and I expect you realise that there is not only this room on the ground floor."

She started to count on her fingers.

"There is the drawing room, the dining room, the ballroom, the refreshment room next to it, the music room, the Chapel and the library not to mention the tapestry room and the room where we have just had breakfast!"

David held up his hands.

"Now you are scaring me, but we will manage them all in time. I am only trying to speed up what we have to do so we don't waste any time searching somewhere like the ballroom where I am certain no one would want to hide anything."

"One never knows what people'll do when they're a bit funny in the head," observed Nanny gloomily.

"You have forgotten the gun room, my Lord," said Newman. "It's big enough for a man to hide any amount of secrets in the cupboards and drawers."

"I will leave that to you, Newman," smiled David. "Meanwhile Miss Benina and I are intending to work very hard and the only person who will not be concerned with looking for the money is Nanny."

"I knows you'll do better if your tummies are full," muttered Nanny, "and that's what they're a-going to be."

"I am already looking forward to luncheon, Nanny. Now come on, Benina, let's start work!"

"I was thinking what a lot of rooms we have to do."

Benina had not exaggerated.

David found that on the first floor there were not only the Master Suites and twelve State rooms, there were fifteen other bedrooms as well as the picture gallery, the china room and a large room that contained the armour and the robes of each succeeding Marquis.

There were also, which David found interesting and he could not help lingering over, a room filled with stuffed wild animals and birds.

There were heads of tigers, black bears, stags and panthers and many weird and unusual stuffed birds. They were exhibited on tables or hanging down from the ceiling.

"I call these fascinating," David said to Benina.

"I felt so too when I first saw them, my Lord, but these birds are not heavy enough to have coins inside them and I am sure you would not wish to open them up."

"That would be sacrilege. Let's go on."

The picture gallery boasted pictures he knew were of inestimable value if they were put onto the open market and the china had been collected by early Marchionesses of Inglestone who had superbly good taste.

It was impossible not to finger some Japanese china figurines and the early English models were very colourful.

"Come along, my Lord, you are wasting time," said Benina when he had stopped for quite five minutes looking at a cabinet full of Russian snuff boxes, ornamented with portraits of the Czars in enamel surrounded by diamonds.

They went into the Master Suite and David was not hopeful there would be a special safe where his grandfather could have deposited his money.

Most private safes, he thought, were too small and the amount of money the Marquis had withdrawn from the Bank would not have fitted into any one he had ever seen.

There was in fact no safe in the Master Suite.

They searched through the cupboards, the cabinets and the drawers and they even looked on top of the canopy over the bed.

There was no sign of even a sixpence anywhere.

They stopped for luncheon and ate hurriedly.

Actually they were both hungry as moving furniture about was much more tiring than even David had expected.

He had somehow suspected his grandfather might have hidden some paper money behind the pictures in the picture gallery, but, although some of them needed repair, there was no sign of any notes.

Also the Bank Manager had said that a great deal of the money his grandfather had taken away was in the form of golden guineas and they would require a large amount of space to hide them.

They had finished most of the first floor by teatime, and there were still a number of ordinary bedrooms which they had not yet investigated.

"Now what we are going to do," David said as they took tea in the study, "is to go and look at the horses, and see if we can possibly go riding tomorrow morning."

"Oh, could we possibly ride?" asked Benina.

"I need exercise and fresh air after spending so long in those stuffy rooms that have not been opened for years."

"They were rather smelly," laughed Benina. "And I suppose you know you have now got white hair!"

David turned round to look at himself in the mirror.

It was quite true.

The dust from the cupboards he had opened and the shelves he had inspected had fallen on his head and he now might have been a man nearing sixty.

"I tell you what I am going to do," he suggested suddenly, "I am going to swim in the lake."

"Do you really think it's warm enough, my Lord? I thought of swimming in the summer, but felt it might have annoyed his Lordship. So I had to be content with carrying water upstairs to have a bath and I found it very tiring."

"Now we will swim in the lake, and I will race you, so at least we are warmed up before we jump in."

Benina thought this a splendid idea, so she hurried upstairs to find Nanny and ask for her best bathing dress.

"You've grown a bit since you last wore it," Nanny said, "so I thinks it'll be a bit tight on you."

"Tight or not, I cannot swim naked!"

However they found that the bathing dress, although somewhat dilapidated like the rest of her clothes, fitted her as she had grown so thin.

Nanny gave her a big bath towel to throw over her shoulders.

She ran downstairs to find David, also with a towel over his shoulders, half-way down to the lake.

As she caught up with him, panting a little because she had run so quickly, he remarked,

"The last time I bathed in India it was even hotter in the water than it was outside!"

"I don't think you will say that now, my Lord."

Actually the water in the lake was not too cold.

They were regarded angrily by a mallard duck, who collected all her babies and swam away indignantly to the other side of the lake.

David was surprised to find that Benina could swim well and strongly for a woman, as he was used to women in India wearing elegant bathing clothes who could seldom do more than stand in the water up to their waists – hoping that the men would be lost in admiration for their elegant but *décolleté* suits.

Benina not only swam beside him but splashed him with water.

She laughed when he complained she was blinding him and he ducked her.

They enjoyed their swim and then wrapped in bath towels they walked back towards the house.

"I feel better after that, Benina, and if we can ride tomorrow I will feel better still."

"Ben said it will not be too soon for the horses. He has been so kind in looking after them. If it had not been for him, they would have both died like the other two."

"On my instructions he has been feeding them the finest oats and if we take them gently, I think that it will be good for their legs."

"And good for us too!" exclaimed Benina. "I used to sneak out and ride whenever I could. But I was always afraid that the Marquis would think that the horses were an extravagance, even after they had been put out to grass, and have them destroyed."

"The more I hear about my grandfather, the more I am convinced he was completely and absolutely crazy. In any well conducted country he would have been certified and put into an asylum!"

"Everyone was far too frightened to suggest that for anyone so grand, and I think you forget how important you are now and there is no one to tell you but Nanny and me."

David laughed loudly.

"I don't feel at all important at present, but I am perfectly prepared, once I find all those millions, to be very overbearing and autocratic!"

Benina shook her head.

"I don't believe you could ever be like that. Nanny says you are the kindest man she has ever met and what she calls 'a real gentleman'."

"Now that *is* praise. The whole trouble in the world today is that there are not enough nannies to teach all the men to be the gentlemen they should be."

He was pondering that no gentleman would have behaved like his grandfather unless he really was mad and did not know what he was doing.

All through the history of the family there had been Inglestones who had become distinguished Generals and Statesmen.

It was only his grandfather who in his dotage had behaved in such a lunatic fashion.

If they were lucky enough to find what they were seeking, he would have to make the family name as famous and as respected as it had been in the past.

Everyone was tired after a delicious dinner and, as they left the dining room where Newman had arranged for them to eat for the first time, David announced,

"I am now retiring to bed."

"I have received strict instructions from Nanny that is what I am to do too. I only wish before we go, we could celebrate having found the treasure."

"There are still some rooms we have not looked at on the first floor, but I am not very optimistic."

Benina gave a deep sigh.

"I feel the same, my Lord."

"If we could only get some form of guidance to tell us where to look. If some of the money was in notes, he would not have hidden it in the garden, so it must be in the house somewhere."

He was thinking as he spoke that the house was as large as an Army barracks and it could take months, if not years, to search it from top to bottom.

"I will pray very hard before I go to sleep tonight," suggested Benina, "but I do think we have done something wrong that we ought to put right first."

"What can that be?"

"We have not yet looked in the Chapel, my Lord. When I first saw it, it looked very unused and empty."

She glanced round at David a little nervously as if she thought he might resent what she was saying.

Then she continued,

"I think because what we have to find will help not only ourselves, but so many others, we should have prayed in the Chapel and perhaps made an offering, as people in ancient times used to do before they went into battle."

"I know what you are saying, Benina, and I am sure you are right. I have never been particularly religious in the fullest sense of the word, but when I was in desperate danger in India and it seemed absolutely impossible for me to come out alive, I prayed to God."

"Of course you did, as we all do – "

Benina paused for a moment before she added,

"Mama and I both prayed very hard that we would be able to stay here at Ingle Hall after we had first arrived, and your grandfather told us to go away."

"I just cannot imagine how he could have been so unpleasant," David responded almost beneath his breath.

"I prayed despairingly, my Lord, for Mama's sake that we would be allowed to stay, and finally, although it was so very difficult, *we did*."

Her voice rose as she went on,

"And now because you have come and everything is very different, I think that I must give a thank-offering, and you must say a special prayer that God will send his angel to show us where the money is hidden."

David thought this a rather touching idea.

"Yes, of course we will. So let's go and look at the Chapel now and see what we can do with it."

They walked down the long corridor on the ground floor which led towards the billiard room and just before they reached it, there was a turning that led down a narrow passage to the Chapel.

It was very old and Benina had read that it had been built at the same time as the main part of Ingle Hall.

As it was not yet dark David thought it unnecessary for them to take a candle or a lantern with them.

They opened the door that felt stiff.

The last rays of the evening sun were still shining through the stained-glass windows.

There were several cracks in the windows, but they did not detract in the slightest way from the beauty of the Chapel which was perfectly proportioned.

With its oak carved pews and marble altar, it was outstandingly beautiful.

Needless to say the floor and the pews were thick with dust and yet, although it was so neglected, it still had, Benina thought, an atmosphere of Holiness about it.

The gold cross on the altar seemed to shine through the dust and the six candlesticks needed polishing yet they were all in place.

For a moment David and Benina just stood in the doorway.

Then, as they moved a little further into the Chapel, Benina knelt down on a prie-dieu directly in front of the altar.

For a moment David hesitated before joining her.

He prayed, as he had prayed at his father's funeral, that he would be as happy and successful in his life as his father had been in his.

He had not taken his place as a titled Englishman as had been expected of him, but had travelled over the world making friends in every country he visited, leaving people happier because they had met him – and at the same time developing himself into a gentleman who could honestly state that he had lived his life to the full.

'That is what I want,' David thought to himself.

Yet he knew that since he had become the Marquis of Inglestone, he bore far greater responsibilities than his father ever had.

He had to do something for the people who relied on the estate and the family of which he was now the Head.

If nothing else, he must set a good example to those who would come after him.

He felt his prayer was finished and glanced round at Benina.

She had closed her eyes, but she had not bent her head – in fact she had thrown it back a little, as if she was looking up into the sky where she believed that God was listening to her, with her hands pressed together in the age-old attitude of prayer.

It suddenly struck David that he had never seen a woman look more beautiful when she was praying.

For that matter he had not seen any woman praying as Benina was praying now.

It had been compulsory in India for the Officers on duty to attend Church Parade on Sunday in Calcutta, Simla or anywhere else they were stationed.

It was a most formal occasion and the women were dressed up in their best and there was always a flutter of elegant hats trimmed with flowers, feathers and veils.

Benina's fair hair after her swim was slightly damp and hanging down her back.

Her lovely face, David considered, was the face of an innocent and a very lovely angel and nothing could be more perfect for her than the background of the Chapel.

As he stood looking down at her, Benina became conscious of his stare.

Opening her eyes, she rose from the prie-dieu and just as a child might have done, she slipped her hand into David's.

They walked out of the Chapel together and when he had closed the heavy door behind him, David said,

"You are quite right, we will have the place cleaned and tidied as soon as possible. Then we will ask the Vicar to visit us and say a special prayer and bless the Chapel as it must have been blessed when it was first built."

Benina's fingers tightened on his.

"I just knew you would understand and when we find the hidden coins, you must place the first ones on the altar and then they will be dedicated to God because he has helped us."

"We will certainly do so and a great deal more, but we have to find the coins first and the rest of the money."

He considered that it would really be a much harder job than he had anticipated – in fact he was beginning to be afraid they were going the wrong way about their quest.

Yet he could not think of another way.

He had not spoken, but because Benina knew what he was thinking, she suggested,

"You must not feel depressed or worried. Now that we have prayed, I am quite, quite certain that because you want the money for the village, the estate and your family as well as for yourself, we *will* find it!"

"I hope you are right, Benina. I felt so optimistic this morning, after what Newman had said, that we would find it in my grandfather's bedroom. We searched every drawer and cupboard."

"Maybe he was anxious not to make it too obvious, and his bedroom would be the place for a burglar to go."

"I suppose you are right. Of course we have a great many more rooms to search, and I am sure Newman turned out the study while we were upstairs."

"He is such a very nice man," sighed Benina, "and so happy to be back here again."

She looked up at David and smiled.

"You see you are making everyone very happy, my Lord. Nanny said this morning it is just like old times to be working with a gentleman again."

David laughed.

"That is the highest compliment I can be paid!"

"Of course it is, my Lord, Nanny has always said 'a lady does not do it in that way', or 'he behaves like a real gentleman.' And that in her estimation is *you*."

"I only hope I can live up to it!"

Benina took her hand from his.

"Now we must retire, as we are both exhausted."

"I know."

They walked slowly upstairs side by side.

As David was undressing he wondered if perhaps his grandfather was watching him from wherever he might be and as he saw his reflection in the mirror, he wondered if he had any resemblance to him.

'At least we are of the same blood,' he mused, 'and he should help rather than hinder me in finding what I am seeking. After all, he has not been able to take it with him, and it is no use to him now in whatever world he is in.'

Then he told himself his grandfather was unlikely to be thinking in such a strange way.

But everything had been very strange since he had gone to Government House expecting to be congratulated on what he had achieved at Fort Tibbee.

Instead his own world had been turned topsy-turvy and he had left for England that very night.

He had a sudden longing for India and the men with whom he had served as a soldier.

He wanted the thrills, excitement and danger of *The Great Game*.

And then he told himself he was being very selfish.

All he should be concerned with was the extremely important position he now held if only he could afford to maintain it.

'*If*' was the operative word.

Everything now depended on finding the money his grandfather had hidden.

He thought it slightly odd that he had gone to the Chapel with Benina to pray that they might find anything so unholy as *money*.

Yet that money, if he did find it, could help a great number of people and provide the employment that was so urgently needed by many loyal workers, besides enabling him to take on the duties that were part of the title he now owned.

He could see the whole story unfolding in front of him almost as if out of a picture and yet nothing could be put into operation without money.

Money had suddenly overnight become something so much more important in his life than it had ever been before.

His father had done what he wanted to do and never worried about money, yet on his death the burden of being without any had fallen on him.

'So far,' he told himself sharply, 'I have not been very successful.'

As he finished his undressing, he gazed at the great four-poster bed where his grandfather had slept and died.

He felt almost as if he was still there and he wanted to shout at him for help and to tell him, as if he was alive, that he could not continue allowing Ingle Hall and all his people to suffer.

'Wherever you are,' David muttered silently, 'you must have the sense to appreciate that something must be done. Someone has to put straight the mess you have made and that unfortunately is me.'

"Tell me, Grandpapa," he called out aloud, "where you have hidden it! For once be kind and decent, and tell me the truth!"

His voice seemed to echo round the room and come back to him.

A little ashamed of himself David climbed into bed.

*

Much of the next morning they spent having a very enjoyable but quiet ride, not wishing to overtax the horses.

After an early luncheon, they resumed their search of the rooms on the first floor, but again without success.

After going to his bedroom to tidy himself for tea, David was walking downstairs when he heard a carriage draw up outside the front door which they had left ajar.

He could see a large elegant carriage drawn by two black horses with two servants on the box that had come to a standstill.

He wondered who on earth it could possibly be and supposed it must be callers, the last thing he needed at the moment.

He hurried down the stairs and almost ran along the corridor to the study.

He opened the door to find that Benina was already there having changed into a pretty red dress and was sitting beside the tea table.

She looked up as he entered.

"You have taken such a long time, my Lord, and I am eating the chocolate cake that Nanny has made for us. If you do not hurry there will be nothing left!"

"I think we have a visitor, Benina."

"Oh no! We don't want one yet, do we?"

"No, of course not, I expect it is some inquisitive neighbours who have heard I have arrived. I can only hope that Newman will have the good sense to turn them away."

"I am sure he will. Here is your tea."

She held out the cup to him.

As David took it from her, the door opened.

"Miss Stella Ashworth," Newman announced in his most authoritarian voice.

CHAPTER SIX

For a moment David was stunned into silence.

Then as Stella saw him, she ran forward.

"David, *darling*!" she cried. "*I am here*! Are you pleased to see me?"

She threw herself against him and he could not help putting an arm round her, but did not kiss her.

He merely looked down at her and asked,

"What has happened? Why are you in England?"

"Papa had to attend an urgent interview at the War Office and I decided to come along with him. How could you leave India without saying goodbye to me?"

"I thought I did and that you understood."

"I do not know what you are talking about, David. Of course I did not understand. But it is wonderful to see you, although I expected you to be in London."

"So you drove down here?" he asked as if he was working it out.

He had taken his arm from her and yet Stella was still standing close to him with her hands flat on his chest.

"I *had* to see you," she whispered, "you know I had to see you."

David became aware that Benina was watching in wide-eyed astonishment.

He deliberately moved away from Stella, saying,

"I want you to meet my cousin who is living here with me. Benina Falcon – Stella Ashworth."

Stella took one quick look at Benina and nodded to her disinterestedly.

Benina, who had half-risen from her chair to shake hands, sat down again.

"May I pour you a cup of tea?" she asked. "I am sure you must need one after your journey from London."

"I am in no hurry," Stella replied almost rudely.

As she spoke the door opened and Newman came in with a teacup and plate for the new arrival.

David picked up his cup of tea.

"It is certainly a surprise to see you, Stella. Now how long will you be staying in London?"

She looked at him coyly from under her eyelashes, before she answered.

"I think that really depends on you – "

"Then I must disappoint you, Stella, as I just cannot come to London at the moment. As you may be aware, my grandfather has died and there is an enormous amount to be done in this house and on the estate. I have no time for gallivanting."

"I am not asking you to gallivant," replied Stella, "but to be with *me*."

"I am afraid that is impossible and I am sorry to tell you that your journey here has been fruitless."

Stella looked towards the window.

"It's growing late, and I think Papa would not wish me to drive back alone in the dark. I brought my lady's maid with me, so I will be no trouble and we can leave, if that is what you want me to do, tomorrow morning."

David realised from the way she was speaking that it would be impossible for him to insist that she drove back to London that night.

He looked despairingly at Benina, who suggested,

"I will go and prepare a bedroom for your friend and Nanny will arrange for the lady's maid to stay in one of the rooms that have been cleaned."

She rose from her chair without finishing the cake she was eating and slipped out of the room before David could open the door for her.

When she thought Benina was out of earshot, Stella enquired,

"Is that badly dressed girl really your relative?"

"You heard me say her name is Falcon, which was my mother's name before she married my father."

Stella gave a rather affected yawn.

"I do find relatives *such* a bore. It must be tiresome for you having her living here in the house."

"As a matter of fact she has been extremely useful to me," David replied coldly. "There is so much to do, as you can already see. My grandfather allowed this house to deteriorate badly before he died."

"Why didn't you tell me your grandfather had died? When the Viceroy told Papa you had left because you had become the Marquis of Inglestone, I couldn't believe it."

The way she was looking at him and the manner in which she spoke told David what he already suspected.

If she had realised when he asked her to marry him that he was already a Marquis she would not have hesitated to accept him.

He was already feeling rather suspicious about her statement that her father had to visit the War Office and it was, he was sure, a fabrication to hide their real reason for coming to England.

David, holding his tea in his hand, did not sit back down on the chair he had been sitting in.

It was too close to Stella.

Instead he sat on the sofa by the tea table.

He had only just put his cup and saucer down on the table when Stella moved to sit next to him.

She slipped her arm through his and let her head rest on his shoulder.

"I was very unhappy when you left, darling David," she breathed. "I knew that I had made a *terrible* mistake in refusing you when you asked me to be your wife."

For a moment David was at a loss for words and then he remarked,

"I feel now as if that happened a long time ago. I have had so much to do since I returned that I have not had a minute to think about my private life."

"Then let me think of it for you," Stella murmured. "I love you, David, and I always have – "

David was wondering desperately what he should say when the door opened and Benina came back.

Instinctively Stella moved a little way from him.

"Newman is taking your luggage upstairs," Benina told Stella. "Your maid says that you have the key of your trunk and she needs to unpack your evening dress."

Stella made a sound which David knew was one of annoyance. She had left her bag in the chair where she had been sitting and she rose from the sofa to retrieve it.

Quickly David rose to his feet.

"I had better fetch a bottle of claret from the cellar," he said to Benina. "I suppose you have told Nanny that Miss Ashworth will be here for dinner."

"I expect Newman has told her and I will help her if she needs me."

She would have left, but David stopped her.

"Wait a minute, Benina, I will fetch the key, then I will come with you."

"I expect Newman can find the claret in the cellar if I give him the key."

David realised she did not appreciate that the last thing he wanted was to be left alone with Stella.

He knew by the way Benina was speaking that she was not only surprised at Stella's affectionate attitude but upset by it.

He could understand why.

She was afraid that she and Nanny might have to leave if Stella was to take her place in helping him restore Ingle Hall.

David, however, was quite determined to have his own way.

He found the key to the cellar in the writing desk and without saying anything to Stella, he then hurried after Benina as she walked down the corridor.

When he caught up with her, he told her,

"There was nothing I could do, but agree to Miss Ashworth staying the night."

"It will be nice for you to have a friend," Benina replied, "and, of course, I will have dinner in the kitchen with Nanny."

"You will do nothing of the sort, I want you to dine with me and that is exactly what you *will* do."

"I am sure you would much rather be alone with her, my Lord."

"It is my decision, Benina, and I will be extremely angry if you do not do as I tell you!"

She looked at him and he recognised that she was bewildered and did not follow what was happening.

"I will explain everything to you later when she has gone. At the same time as far as she is concerned, you are the hostess. You are to do as I tell you and come down to dinner and stay afterwards until we all retire to bed."

Benina did not reply, but he knew when he left her to go to the cellar that she would obey his instructions.

He gave the claret to Newman and after a moment's thought, he went into the kitchen.

As he expected, Nanny was making something on the kitchen table and Benina had sat down opposite her.

David deliberately closed the kitchen door as if he did not want to be overheard.

Then going nearer to Nanny, he asked,

"You have heard what has happened?"

"I understands we have a visitor, my Lord."

"An unexpected one and an unwanted one. Now I need your help and this is very important."

He looked at Benina as he spoke and he was aware that she was listening with a worried look in her eyes.

"The last thing that I could possibly want now is for Miss Ashworth to suspect that we are searching the house for my grandfather's money and that we have practically none until we find it.

"There is no gossip like Indian gossip – they chatter and chatter away when they have nothing else to do. Miss Ashworth's father is the General Commandant in Calcutta, and he was therefore told by the Viceroy why I had come home. But they know nothing else about my position here or the difficulties we are involved in."

Nanny gave a sigh.

"I gets it, my Lord, and it'd be a great mistake for them to talk, as they surely would if they knew the full truth."

"I knew you would, Nanny, and Benina must help me tonight over dinner. It is going to be very difficult if Miss Ashworth asks any awkward questions."

Benina's eyes lit up.

"Of course, I will help. I did not understand and I thought you wanted to be alone with her."

"I think, without meaning to sound too conceited," continued David, "she wants to be alone with me, but I am apprehensive at the questions I may have to answer. Thus I need you. You must keep the conversation rolling so that she is not suspicious in any way."

"I do follow you now," said Benina. "I am sorry if I was being stupid."

"As she will undoubtedly be tired from travelling, I am sure we can go to bed early without seeming rude."

"I will yawn when you tell me to, my Lord!"

Now she was laughing and David hesitated for a second before saying,

"I think you might suggest that she would like to rest before dinner. Then if we go back and finish our tea, there will not be such a long wait between the two meals."

Benina seemed indecisive.

"Now you do what his Lordship requires," Nanny came in. "I knows better than you how these smart ladies, wherever they be, in Mayfair or India, talk their heads off and poke their noses into things what don't concern them. 'Least said, soonest mended,' as my old father would say."

"Quite right, Nanny," agreed David. "Now come on Benina, let's go back and I am sure that we can keep the conversation going on India if nothing else!"

He saw that the worried expression had gone from Benina's face.

She jumped to her feet eagerly.

"Tell Miss Ashworth," said Nanny, "I've shown the lady's maid up to her room and one for herself."

"I hope she will be comfortable."

"We've done our best, my Lord, and if there's too much dust, she'll feel she's back in India!"

David was chuckling as he and Benina walked back to the study.

When Stella came down for dinner after being more or less forced into having a rest, David had to admit that she did look exceedingly glamorous.

She was wearing a gown that would have been a lot more suited to a formal dinner at Government House than, as she had intended, a *tête-à-tête* with him.

The full skirt made it possible to have row after row of lace-trimmed frills reaching from the waist to the floor, and the same frills covered her arms and accentuated the smallness of Stella's waist.

She wore rather too much jewellery for a young girl and David suspected that she had worn it deliberately.

She wanted to show him how beautiful she would look at the Opening of Parliament in the Inglestone jewels.

These were in the safe in the pantry and he had not even bothered to look at them as he knew that Newman had looked after them carefully and David was certain he would have told him if anything was missing.

They had been entailed for longer than anything else and included a necklace that had been given by Queen Elizabeth to the then Marquis of Inglestone.

Compared to Stella's, Benina's dress was out-of-date and plain, although dear Nanny had done her best by adding a dashing sash of blue satin, the colour of her eyes.

She looked, David pondered, very young and very unsophisticated.

At the same time 'beautiful' was the right word to describe her.

'One day,' he mused, 'I must give her a dress that is as expensive as Stella's to frame her beauty as she should be framed – '

With a sigh he recalled that it entirely depended on whether they found his grandfather's money.

He had changed into evening dress for the first time since he had come back to Ingle Hall.

It would have seemed out of place when they were eating at a small table in the study, but correct for a formal occasion in the dining room.

Newman had risen to the moment.

There were four magnificent silver candlesticks on the table as well as a huge ornamental goblet that was three hundred years old.

The pictures round the wall were all of the previous Marquises of Inglestone by a great artist of the day. The earliest were now of enormous value, although they could all have done with extensive cleaning.

Despite Newman's tireless efforts there was still a good covering of dust on the panelling, but David thought it was unlikely that Stella would notice it.

As she settled herself into a chair on his right, she looked around her appraisingly.

"This is a marvellous room for a party," she cooed. "I am sure we could easily seat fifty or sixty people here!"

David was well aware that she used the word '*we*'.

"I have always disliked large parties, but I believe my great-grandfather gave one each year that was always followed by a ball."

"I did so miss dancing with you, David, when you disappeared so unexpectedly."

Stella spoke in a low seductive voice that he knew only too well – it was the same way all the pretty women in Simla had spoken to him and he had found it amusing to flirt with them as they expected him to do.

Now David commented rather quickly,

"I have been far too busy to even think of balls and parties. In point of fact, Benina and I are worried that the fields have been neglected and no crops have been sown for several years."

He hoped that Stella would be bored into silence, but instead she persisted,

"After you had gone, Papa learnt what a wonderful job you had done when you saved Fort Tibbee. Everyone in Calcutta was talking about your exploits and saying how clever and brave you were."

"I hope they were doing nothing of the sort – "

"But of course they were, David, and, as Papa said, it was a great triumph for those in *The Great Game* that the Russians had been foiled once again."

David drew in his breath.

"I am sure," he retorted almost angrily, "that your father has told you never to talk about *The Great Game* or those who take part in it."

Stella laughed.

"He told me to be careful what we said in Calcutta. But of course people realised that you were the hero of the hour and had been praised by the Viceroy. Papa said that if your bravery had not been on a secret mission, you would have been awarded a medal."

She gave a little laugh and added,

"But now you have a large Coronet on your head you really don't need one!"

David did not reply, thinking how dangerous this

sort of conversation was – it was in fact typical of stupid women who had no idea of what those who served in *The Great Game* went through.

Once again he tried to turn the conversation round, but Stella could not be silenced.

"When I learnt that you had gone," she was saying, "I could not believe it was true. For a moment I was afraid the Russians had caught up with you and were determined to murder you because you had saved the Fort."

"It is something I do not wish to talk about," David responded sharply.

"You are too modest, darling!"

She put out her hand and laid it on his arm.

"You must allow all those who love you to say how proud they are of everything you have done for India. But, now you are so distinguished, I feel sure Her Majesty will want to keep you in England."

He did not answer and after a moment she added,

"I can see there is a lot to be done to this house and of course we must employ the best architect – "

"How long is your father staying here in England?" David asked her abruptly.

Stella hesitated and then she answered,

"I will answer that question – when we are alone."

David knew the answer without being told and for a moment he could not think of anything to say.

Then because she was determined to help, Benina very tactfully begged Stella to tell her about the Viceroy's house in Calcutta.

"I have always heard it resembles Kedleston Hall that was redesigned by the Adam brothers," she persisted. "They also worked on various parts of this house and made the furniture in the drawing room and I will show it to you after dinner."

"I want to see everything," said Stella. "Especially the ballroom where my father said he had once danced as a young subaltern and thought it one of the most beautiful ballrooms he had ever seen."

"I will show it to you," offered Benina.

Stella gave her a rather sour look.

"I think that David should show me as he is such a wonderful dancer that I am sure that even without a band we might waltz round the room as we have done so often."

There was little David could do to stop her making such remarks and she was continually touching him with her hand.

It was something he had always disliked, whoever the woman was, but he found that it was an essential part of their flirting.

Fortunately they were served only three courses for dinner and although Nanny had cooked them very well, she had not expected there to be a third person for dinner and so the helpings were inevitably rather small.

There was an inaudible sigh of relief from David as dinner ended and when Benina suggested they should go to the study, Stella said to David,

"Come with us. You cannot sit here drinking alone and you know I am longing to talk to you."

"As a matter of fact, Stella, I am going to bed very early. I have a great deal to do tomorrow and Benina and I have to pay a visit to a farm on the other side of the estate, so we will breakfast early."

"Would you like me to come too?" asked Stella.

David shook his head.

"It is extremely rough riding and we only have two horses. I think you would be wise to set off for London as early as possible as the traffic into the City often becomes heavy in the afternoon."

"I don't want to go back to London," she protested petulantly.

"But I am afraid that is just what you will have to do, because quite frankly we are not ready for visitors yet. As you can see we have a very small staff and I have not yet had time to put my grandfather's affairs in order."

There was nothing Stella could say and they walked into the study in silence.

They sat down and it was quite obvious that Stella resented Benina being there and to make matters worse as far as she was concerned, David deliberately sat down at his writing desk.

He said there was so much he had to do and thus they must forgive him for not joining in the conversation.

Finally, after a long uncomfortable silence David said that he was going to bed.

"Benina and I have had a hard day and I am sure that after your journey, Stella, you will be glad of an early night."

She then objected that she was not tired, but David would not listen.

Eventually they walked rather stiffly up the stairs.

The room Nanny had prepared for Stella was one of the finest of the State rooms with silver and gold furniture.

Stella's lady's maid was waiting for her and David wished her goodnight at the door.

"Sleep well, Stella, it was very kind of you to come and visit me. You and your father must come to stay when the house is in order and I can entertain you properly."

"You know I only wanted to see *you*," murmured Stella softly.

He left her and went towards the Master suite and when they reached Benina's bedroom, she whispered,

"Are we really going out early in the morning?"

"I have left a note for Nanny," David replied, "to say we will have breakfast at seven-thirty and the horses are to be round at eight o'clock. Then we will keep out of sight until she leaves before we come back for the search."

Benina gave a little giggle.

Without saying anything further she closed her door and David walked slowly to his own room.

He was thinking that on the whole the evening had passed off no worse than he expected, but equally he was worried at what Stella had said of the gossip about him in Calcutta.

Then he told himself he was safe enough here.

Yet he remembered that the Russians were reputed never to forget their enemies.

He undressed and then opened the windows wide to let in the cool night air and climbed into bed.

Benina had given him a book she had found in the library on the early history of the Inglestone family.

It was rather difficult to read as it was old and the print was bad, yet because the book was so interesting, he had managed to read nearly a chapter every night.

With two candles by his bed he was just beginning where he had left off when the door opened.

To his astonishment Stella walked in.

For a moment he could not see her clearly and then as she reached his bed, he saw that her hair was flowing over her shoulders.

She was wearing a very attractive negligee that was open down the front to show the nightgown beneath it.

"*Stella!*" he cried. "What are you doing here?"

She sat down on the side of his bed facing him as she answered,

"I have to talk to you, darling, and it is impossible when that tiresome young girl is always with us."

David put his book down on the table beside him.

"There is nothing to say, Stella, you told me very clearly you did not love me, and I came home determined to forget you."

"But I am sure you were unable to, dearest David, just as I was unable to forget you."

She moved nearer to him holding out her arms.

"Kiss me, David, kiss me like you used to kiss me. You will find our love is even more wonderful than it has ever been."

David did not move and then he muttered,

"*No*, Stella. What is over is over and it is no use trying to go back."

"I do love you, David, as I will always love you. It was only because I was afraid of poverty that I was foolish enough to say 'no'."

"You were quite right. We should not have been happy together, I recognise that now."

"But I realise now that I do love you desperately, so we can be married and Papa is delighted at the idea."

David thought cynically that he was not surprised.

It was a very different issue for the General to give the Marquis of Inglestone permission to marry his daughter than to accept a young Captain with no money and no title!

Stella moved even closer to him.

He put out his hands to stop her coming any nearer.

"Now listen, Stella, you have no right to come here,

as you well know. I have no intention at all of ruining your reputation, so that your father can insist on our marriage."

He knew from the flicker of Stella's eyelashes that was just what she had been planning.

"Go back to your room now, Stella, and forget we ever thought we were in love with each other."

"But I love you, David," she cried. "Kiss me and tell me you will no longer say these unkind words to me."

"As I have told you, I have no intention of ruining your reputation," David repeated sharply. "Return to your own room, and you must leave for London early tomorrow morning."

Stella stared at him.

"Are you really saying this to me?" she demanded.

"I am saying it and I *mean* it."

Stella rose from the bed and onto her feet.

"I have offered you my heart, David, and you have refused it. I don't believe that you would have forgotten so quickly, if it had not been for that girl you pretend is your relative. Very well then, I hope she satisfies you with her dowdy clothes and her ignorance of the Social world!"

She stamped her foot, but it was not very effective as she was wearing bedroom slippers.

"I hate you, David," she screamed. "I hate you for what you have done to me and I will *never* forgive you."

She reached the door, pulled it open and then made her parting shot.

"I hope after all you have done to me, the Russians will get you!"

With that she stormed out of the room and slammed the door behind her.

David gave a deep sigh.

He could hardly believe what had just happened.

He was in fact deeply shocked that Stella, who he had always considered young and innocent, should actually have come to his bedroom and he was quite sure that she had been prepared to stay there with him.

He was used to married women in Calcutta being unfaithful to their husbands, but he had never had anything to do with the young unmarried girls.

He could only think now that he had been so very lucky in escaping from Stella, who he had once foolishly wanted to be his wife.

He knew only too well from past experience that if he married her, she would be unfaithful to him.

Just as so many other women were unfaithful while their husbands were doing their duty for their Queen and country.

These wives were undoubtedly bored with little but female company and yet that was no excuse.

'It is what I have never wanted in my life and what I do not intend to have,' he told himself sternly.

Equally he was sorry that Stella should be so upset, even though he despised her for her behaviour.

He had considered himself in love with her because she was so beautiful and in the atmosphere of India it was difficult for a man not to seek love.

Perhaps love was too perfect a word to describe the emotions that were certainly aroused more by the Indian climate than by anything else.

'I have indeed had a very lucky escape.'

He got out of bed and walked to the window.

Outside the moon was shedding its silver light over the garden and he could see it shimmering on the lake.

It looked so enchanting that for a moment he forgot the difficulties that were confronting him.

He only thought with a feeling of satisfaction it was now his.

"It's mine for my lifetime," he called out aloud.

Then he remembered that it was essential for him to produce a son and heir.

There were so few Ingles left and as far as he knew there was no one to follow in his footsteps as he had just followed in his grandfather's.

'I will have to marry someone,' he pondered.

Then, as he recalled the anger in Stella's face when she left him, he shivered.

He might well be suffering now, yet it was nothing to what he would suffer if he married a woman like her – she would be unfaithful whenever he turned his back and what she called her love for him was really for his title and position in Society.

He looked up at the stars and knew he was asking to be loved for himself – as he had always hoped.

He had believed he would find the ideal woman as his father had done and been blissfully happy, but simply because he had now inherited his grandfather's title, it was unlikely that such a blessing could ever be his.

He turned away from the window.

The moonlight on the garden and lake below was so stunning that he knew it was part of the beauty he craved – the beauty best expressed quite simply by the word '*love*'.

But it was something so many men had found out of reach and only a few had been lucky enough to find love and possess it.

What chance had he?

He pulled the curtains to shut out the moonlight and then he went slowly back to bed.

He felt as if all his dreams had been roughly broken and now the future seemed even more difficult and more hopeless than it had ever been.

*

Benina had heard a door slamming shut sharply and wondered if something was wrong.

She had not got into her bed and although she was undressed she had taken some time in arranging her riding habit on a chair so that it would be ready for her when she awoke in the morning.

Benina knew that she must not keep David waiting as her father always said there was nothing more annoying than unpunctual women, believing it a man's duty to wait for them.

She put her riding boots in front of the chair.

Then she walked over to the window to have a last look at the moonlight.

The garden was a Fairyland and as she gazed down at the lake she thought what fun it had been to swim with David.

'I am so lucky,' she thought. 'If it had been anyone else he might have been as unkind and cruel as the Marquis and sent Nanny and me away from Ingle Hall.'

And how thrilled the pensioners would be at all he had done for them.

She was sure no other man would be so generous when he had so little money.

'He is *wonderful*! Wonderful!' she told herself.

Then she sensed a quiver of jealousy sweep through her – Stella Ashworth was so beautiful and obviously very enamoured with him.

'How could he possibly refuse her?' she wondered.

Then she thought perhaps it was because he was at the moment so poor that he did not want to respond to her affection for him.

She was hoping and praying that Stella would leave as David had told her to do in the morning.

Then a thought suddenly struck Benina.

When he found his money, he would then feel he could accept Stella Ashworth's advances.

The whole idea was agonising.

It was like a dagger into her heart to think that she would lose David.

She clenched her fingers together and the pain was an echo of the pain in her chest.

It was then she finally admitted to herself that she loved David.

She had loved him since she had first seen him.

It was not only because he was so very handsome, but because he was so kind and understanding and he was so good to Nanny and to poor old Newman.

'No other man could be so marvellous,' she mused.

Then once again she could see Stella's seductive eyes flashing at him, her long fingers touching his arm and naturally she wanted to dance with him.

It was what Benina herself would love to do.

Because her feelings were growing more and more intense, she turned away from the window.

'I must go to bed,' she decided, 'and try to sleep. It will be difficult when perhaps David is thinking of the beautiful Miss Ashworth – '

She knew it was almost wicked, but she could not help hoping that they would not find the money too soon as if they did, David could then ask Stella to marry him.

Perhaps he would give her and Nanny a cottage in the village.

'I will have to leave – I could not stay,' she felt.

The idea of it seemed to tear her heart into shreds.

She walked back resolutely towards her bed as she must have all her wits about her tomorrow.

As she reached her bed she heard a door slam and because it seemed very loud in the silence, she ran to her own door.

She pulled it open.

By the light of the one candle burning in the silver sconce in the passage she saw Stella.

She was disappearing into the room that Nanny had prepared for her.

She slammed that door too, but not as loudly.

Benina stood staring at the closed door.

She realised, although it seemed incredible, that the first door she had heard slam had been the one belonging to the Master Suite.

It was obvious that Stella had come from there.

'She must,' Benina reckoned, 'have gone in to say goodnight to David and what he said annoyed her and she had then rushed back to her room in a temper.'

Benina had no idea what had happened or what had upset her, she only knew with a lift of her heart that David could not have been affectionate or kind to Stella.

Otherwise she would not have been so angry.

Suddenly Benina felt happy again.

She admitted to herself that she had been depressed and uneasy ever since Stella's arrival.

But now her heart seemed to be dancing around and the sun was shining in her heart.

She did not quite understand the whole scenario.

But as she lay down on her bed, she closed her eyes and whispered softly,

"Thank You, God. *Thank You.*"

CHAPTER SEVEN

The next morning Benina was dressed and tidying her hair when the door opened and David peeped in.

He did not speak to her, but merely beckoned with his hand and she knew he was going downstairs.

She ran over the bedroom, picked up her riding hat and followed him.

He arrived at the ground floor and instead of going out as she expected, he turned towards the breakfast room.

When she joined him, she mumbled to David,

"I thought we would have to creep out of the house without breakfast."

"Newman would be annoyed if we did, Benina, and quite frankly I am feeling hungry."

He helped himself to bacon and eggs and passed a plate to Benina.

"Thank you, my Lord. Where are we going?"

"Anywhere at all as long as we keep away from the house and I suggest we hurry."

She realised he was afraid that Stella would find out that they were leaving and might come down to protest and make a scene.

They ate in silence.

Then, with David leading the way, they hurried out of a back door and on to the stables.

Ben was there and had saddled the two horses.

David lifted her onto the one with a side saddle.

Then as he mounted the other horse, Ben piped up,

"You'll not be rough with 'em, my Lord. They're better than I've ever seen 'em on their new food, but they ain't as strong as them ought to be."

David smiled at him.

"We will be very careful with them, Ben, and thank you for having them ready for us."

Ben touched his forelock and they rode off.

They went first through the paddock at the back of the stables and then onto the fields that should have been growing crops.

It was only as they were riding along with the sun rising in the sky that Benina said,

"I forgot in my hurry to bring my hat."

"There are only the birds and the bees to see you," David remarked, "and they will tell you that you look very attractive."

Benina laughed.

"I am delighted to receive a compliment even from the rabbits if they will offer me one!"

"Well, I can easily pay you a compliment, Benina, by saying you ride extremely well. I know the moment I see a woman on a horse whether she is a good or bad rider and you are undoubtedly at the top of the list."

"It is fabulous to be riding again, my Lord."

She bent forward to pat the neck of her horse.

With the sunlight shining on her hair, David felt she might be a Goddess riding towards Olympus.

They did not talk much, but rode on in the direction he had chosen to what had originally been the Home Farm.

They were not surprised to find the house not only

empty but in a poor condition. Part of the roof had fallen in and everything including the pigsties needed repair.

"You know what this is going to cost," David said after he had looked round for several minutes in silence.

"You will soon be able to repair it or build another Home Farm," commented Benina.

"If we find the money," he said, accentuating '*if*'.

"I am absolutely certain we will – "

They rode on, finding another farmhouse in more or less the same state and of course empty.

It was nearly two o'clock when they arrived back at Ingle Hall.

David insisted on returning by the back route and Benina knew it was because he wanted to be quite certain that Stella Ashworth had left before they entered the house.

She thought that she had never enjoyed a morning more nor been happier than she had been with David.

She waited apprehensively in case he should look worried and depressed, as she thought he was at breakfast.

There was however no sign of Stella's horses in the stables and her carriage was not in the yard.

David walked into the house, not the way they had left it, but through the front door.

Newman was in the hall looking worried.

"I wonders as to what'd happened to your Lordship. Luncheon's been ready for ages and Nanny was worrying it'd be spoilt."

"I am sorry we are late, Newman, but now we are back and very hungry."

He put his hat down on one of the chairs and asked,

"Did Miss Ashworth leave without any trouble?"

There was a slight pause before Newman replied,

"She waited until it were nearly midday, my Lord, hoping you'd return. Then I says to her, I says, that you'd be likely to stay out for luncheon – so she went."

David gave a sigh of relief.

Newman was obviously hesitating, then he added,

"As she steps into the carriage, Miss Ashworth says to me, 'tell his Lordship when he returns that women and Russians have long memories'."

Listening, Benina almost gave a little cry of horror, but she suppressed it in case she should upset David.

He did not say anything.

Newman hurried away to bring in the luncheon. It was rather over-cooked, but they were both ravenous and they ate without speaking.

When they had finished and Newman had left the coffee on the table, David suggested,

"Now we must go back to our work. I want to have another look at the first floor before we start on the second. I cannot help being convinced that is where my grandfather would have hidden his money."

"Before you do that," replied Benina, "I want you to come with me and this is very important."

David looked at her in surprise.

"What is this all about, Benina?"

"I want to show you something."

She got up from the table as she spoke and walked towards the door.

David opened it for her.

"Where do we go now?"

Benina slipped her hand into his.

"Somewhere that you should have gone a long time ago."

She drew him along the passage that led towards the study and then she turned down a long side corridor to a flight of stairs.

It was rather dark and narrow and only as they went along it did David realise they were going to the gun room.

When they entered, he thought it was larger than he remembered.

It contained a collection of sporting-guns, fishing-rods and duelling-pistols as well as other weapons that had been handed down over the ages.

David, like all men, was delighted with them.

"I just cannot think why I didn't come here at once. Look at all these pistols. We must try them out to see if they still work."

"I am sure they will, my Lord, and I will challenge you as to who hits the bull's-eye first!"

David looked at her in surprise.

"Can you shoot?"

"Of course I can. Papa always thought a woman should be able to defend herself. As we lived in the depths of the country, it was a mistake not to anticipate that there might be highwaymen behind a hedge or a dangerous wild animal lurking about."

David laughed.

"I will have to make a list of your many talents, I can see."

"I am afraid there are not very many, and one thing I have never learnt to do is to flirt!"

David thought he might have known she would not have missed the way that Stella had been behaving.

Although it was all too familiar to him, Benina was inexperienced and innocent and how could she know that so many women in the Social world behaved in exactly the same way?

He picked up a modern pistol that was lying on top of a table, guessing that it was one his grandfather must have acquired fairly recently.

To his surprise there were several of them and he wondered if they had been bought as a precaution to deal with burglars who might come to steal the pictures.

Then he vaguely recalled someone saying that his grandfather had threatened to shoot anyone who came to the house whom he did not welcome.

"This is what I brought you here for, my Lord, as I think that after what Miss Ashworth said to Newman, you would be very foolish not to be armed."

He realised she was referring to the Russians and he had to admit it was a sensible idea.

Benina picked up a revolver.

"I will carry this one, my Lord, and I think it would be wise and also kind to give one to Newman."

"Do you think he could manage one?"

"Of course he can, I heard him telling Nanny that if she wanted rabbits or ducks, he would shoot one for her."

"That answers the question," David smiled. "But I think if it is what Newman needs, he had better be armed with a proper gun."

"I should let him choose what he wants," suggested Benina, "and let us all be certain we have enough bullets."

They searched and found them in a drawer.

"Now to work," enthused David.

They walked back up the stairs and as they were passing through the hall, Newman appeared.

"We are going to search again on the first floor, and

by the way, Newman, Miss Benina insists that you and I carry guns or pistols to protect ourselves."

"I've been thinking, your Lordship should do just that," replied Newman, "ever since you've been here. As it so happens, I've got me own gun by me bed, but I'd feel happier if I had something I could carry in me pocket."

"Then help yourself, Newman, but I see no reason why you should be particularly anxious."

He knew this was not strictly true, then as if Benina realised that he did not want to speak about the Russians, she remarked,

"Now you are here people are bound to talk about the picture gallery and there are valuables of some sort in every room."

"Yes, of course," agreed David.

He reached the top of the stairs, so he did not see Benina, halfway up the stairs, look back meaningfully at Newman, who nodded his head.

She was well aware, because Nanny had told her, that Stella's lady's maid had intrigued the kitchen with a graphic description of how David had saved Fort Tibbee.

'I would suppose,' she ruminated as she followed him along the first floor passage, 'that it was far too good a story for anyone to keep secret.'

At the same time she was feeling frightened.

She had read in magazines and newspapers about Russia's ambition to build up a huge Empire as impressive as and even larger than the new German Empire.

Prince Otto von Bismarck, the First Chancellor of the German Empire had succeeded in uniting all the small German Principalities into an Empire.

The Russians were determined to do the same in the Balkans and there was very little doubt that their advances in Asia showed they ultimately desired to take over India.

However, Benina was conscious that David did not want to talk about the Russians.

They worked hard on the first floor moving things, opening endless drawers and cupboards, hunting for secret passages which they never found.

When it was tea-time, they had to wash away the dust and dirt from their hands before they went downstairs.

Nanny as expected had baked a fruit cake and there were several plates with sandwiches, bread and butter and delicious small buns.

David said he had not eaten such delights since he had been in the nursery.

"I shall never be too old for Nanny's little tit-bits," sighed Benina.

David smiled at her.

"You have been a brick today, Benina, but I do not want you to become too tired."

"I am not tired, and I cannot help thinking about the magnificent horses you will be able to buy once you have found the hidden millions."

"I was thinking of that as well. The horses we were riding this morning did us well, but I have a feeling that Ben is going to think they should have a rest tomorrow. It would be a mistake to push them too hard too quickly."

"I agree, my Lord, but I did enjoy riding today."

"I swear to you that we will ride in the future on the finest horses available – once I can pay for them."

He noticed Benina's eyes light up.

He did not realise that it was not only because he was promising her horses.

He was promising her they would be together in the future.

It was impossible for Benina to put into words how relieved she was that Stella Ashworth had finally gone.

Even now she could feel the agony that had swept over her when she thought that David would respond to the seductive way she was speaking and caressing him.

She was not so naïve as not to realise that if David brought a bride to the house, she and Nanny would have to leave.

When tea was finished, Newman appeared to take away the tray.

"It was lovely to have so much silver out," Benina said. "It must have taken you a long time to polish it."

"That's true, Miss Benina, and with everything in the safe as black as the night, it's going to take me a week of Sundays to get it back to the brightness it should have."

"There's plenty of time, so don't exhaust yourself."

David then left the room.

Lowering her voice, Benina muttered to Newman,

"I think we would be wise to carry our guns loaded. If we were burgled or attacked, there might not be time to load them in a hurry."

"I've been thinking of that meself, Miss Benina."

He paused and looked to the door as if to make sure that David was not listening.

Going a little nearer to Benina, he added,

"Seeing as what we've heard about them Ruskies, I've asked Mr. Cosnet and Ben to sleep in the house till we be sure they're not after his Lordship."

"That is a very wise idea of yours. I am sure Nanny will not mind cooking for two extra in the evening."

Newman smiled.

"Mr. Cosnet knows the way to get to Nanny's heart.

He comes in today with a bowlful of strawberries and he's promised her there'll be some raspberries tomorrow!"

"I know that'll please her and I expect we will have some of them for dinner."

"You can bet on that, Miss Benina."

He left just as David returned and Benina thought it would be a mistake to tell him what had been arranged.

She was fully aware how touchy he became when anyone referred to the Russians and had seen how horrified he had been when Stella had said that they were all talking about him in Calcutta.

It also meant, she was sure, that he would be talked about in England too.

Every word made life more dangerous for him.

Because she did not want him to feel depressed, she set out at dinner to be amusing and to keep him laughing.

She told him stories of her father's horses and of the people they had known in the country. She recounted anecdotes about her relatives and some who had been very eccentric in their behaviour.

When they went into the study after dinner, David threw himself down in one of the armchairs.

"I have a lot of work I should do before I go to bed, Benina, but I do want you to go on talking to me, as I have never enjoyed an evening more."

"You are like a child being told fairy stories to send him to sleep," Benina teased him.

"You tell me stories that I find really amusing and I cannot hear too many of them."

They carried on talking until Benina yawned.

"Frankly I am rather tired, so I am going to bed, but don't be late yourself, my Lord."

"I have several letters I should have written more than a week ago to friends who were kind to me in India. I was not able to say goodbye to them as I had left in such a hurry. If I don't write them now, they will never be done."

"Well limit yourself to two or three every night and then the task will not be so arduous."

Benina walked towards the door before she added,

"Let's think where we will start tomorrow. As you know, there must still be nearly half the house to be done."

David threw up his hands.

"I know! I know! I keep hoping and praying that we will find the money soon, so we will not have to look any further."

"I had thought of that already. So hurry and finish your letters. There may soon be many congratulations you will have to answer!"

Benina did not wait for a reply, but closed the door and ran upstairs to her room.

She was really exhausted as well as feeling a little stiff because she had not ridden for so long.

The horses had carried them nobly and she thought good food would make them stronger every day.

At least she and David would have plenty time to ride before they settled down to what looked like being an everlasting search.

She undressed and then she walked to the window to have another look at the moonlight.

She wanted to feel the beauty of it before she went to sleep.

First she looked up at the stars and then down into the garden where there was a fountain on the lawn.

She was contemplating how glorious it would be if

they could make it play again, but as there was so much to do for everyone, she did not dare ask Cosnet for anything more outside the kitchen garden.

She looked out towards a row of lime trees with the moon shimmering like silver on the leaves.

Suddenly she was almost certain that she had seen a movement, but it was too dark to see anything clearly.

Yet she was sure that in the darkness something or someone was moving – slowly like a man moving step by step and pausing between each one.

Still she could not be sure.

Yet she felt as if by instinct that there was danger in the air, whether she could account for it or not.

She turned back into the room.

There was only one candle by the bed and beside it lay the revolver she had carried in her pocket when she had gone downstairs for dinner.

She picked it up.

Then blowing out the candle, she opened the door and ran downstairs.

By this time Newman would have gone to bed and the house was in darkness except for an occasional candle in one of the sconces.

Newman had wanted more candles, but Nanny had said they could not afford them and anyway she had added sharply that no one should be walking about the house after they had all gone to bed.

In her hurry to run downstairs Benina had forgotten to put on her slippers, so she ran barefooted across the hall and down the passage to the study.

When she opened the door, it was to see David still sitting at the writing desk with a pen in his hand.

He looked up at her in surprise.

She shut the door behind her and ran towards him.

"You might think I am being foolish," she panted, "but I am almost certain I saw someone moving in the trees on the far side of the lawn."

She looked up at him, afraid that he would laugh at her and tell her not to be so imaginative.

Instead he muttered,

"If it is anyone looking for me, they will doubtless expect to find me either in my bedroom or in here."

Benina thought for a moment, then she suggested,

"If there is a light downstairs, they will know you have not gone to bed."

"That makes sense, and I am wondering how they will get in."

Benina gave a helpless sigh.

"There are many windows on the ground floor and we both know that most of them are unshuttered and are in such a bad state it would be easy for anyone to open them."

David nodded.

"We will just have to wait and see. You have your revolver with you, Benina?"

"Yes, of course."

As she was holding it down by her side, it had been hidden by her nightgown.

For the first time since she had left her bedroom she remembered that she had not put on her dressing gown – in her fright she had run downstairs only in her nightgown.

It was a pretty one made by Nanny of a soft cotton and it appeared almost like a dress and was not transparent.

All the same Benina blushed because she thought that David was looking at her somewhat critically.

"I am so sorry. I was in such a hurry to reach you, I forgot as I was just getting into bed."

David smiled.

"The way we look is of no importance at present. I suggest we hide behind the curtains which will give us a chance to see anyone who comes into the room before they can see us."

There were two big windows in the study and they went to the one behind the writing desk.

The study was on the same side of the house as her bedroom and David's.

It was not possible for them to see the lime trees where Benina had thought she had seen someone moving. In fact from where they were now there was nothing to see but the lawn and the fountain in the moonlight.

David was intently looking out of the window with his revolver in his right hand and Benina was holding hers.

She felt she could almost hear her heart beating and as she was scared, it seemed to be thundering inside her.

She knew that David was trying to hear if there was the sound of anyone breaking a window or moving about the house.

Newman had closed the windows in the study when he had pulled the curtains, so David put out his hand and very slowly, making no noise, unlatched the window.

Then he pushed it open and the night air rushed in.

They were both listening, but could hear nothing.

CHAPTER EIGHT

Benina felt that David was already thinking that she had been hysterical and unnecessarily scared and she was just about to say she was sorry and would go back to bed.

Then there was just the faintest sound behind them.

They both turned round.

David peeped out of the left side of the curtain and Benina the right.

There was nothing to see by the light of the candles except the room just as they had left it.

Benina noticed that one of the cushions on the sofa looked crushed and Newman must have forgotten to pat it back into shape after he had drawn the curtains.

It was then they heard just the slightest creak of the door being opened.

Benina drew in her breath and she felt sure David was doing the same.

Slowly the door opened just an inch or so.

Then suddenly it was flung forward violently and two men burst into the room.

They were both carrying rifles at the ready.

For a moment David paused.

Then he pulled back the curtain and shot at the man facing him.

He wounded him not in the heart, as it would have killed him, but in the arm that was carrying his rifle.

He gave a loud scream and toppled backwards and his rifle went off as he did so.

The bullet flew upwards towards the ceiling.

It was then, with a swiftness which must have come from a soldier's training, the other man aimed at David.

Before he could pull the trigger Benina aimed her revolver and shot him in the shoulder.

Just as his companion had done, he fell backwards and his rifle went off as he did so with a resounding report.

Next there came a crash from the window as a third assailant burst in behind David and Bernina.

David raised his fist and smashed it into the man's jaw, knocking him to the ground unconscious.

Even as David and Benina came from behind the curtains, Newman and Cosnet were running into the room.

They had obviously not gone to bed as they were both fully dressed and carrying their rifles in their hands.

The men on the floor were groaning and writhing about. Their rifles were lying on the floor beside them.

David took charge at once.

"Take these men to the Police Station immediately. Charge them with breaking and entering here with intent to murder anyone who tried to stop them."

There were broad smiles on the faces of Newman and Cosnet.

Cosnet ran back to the kitchen to fetch ropes.

Looking down at the wounded men as they waited, Benina knew without even hearing them swear in their own language that they were Russians – they were not big men but unpleasant-looking and undoubtedly very strong.

She recognised that if David had not been armed he would have been lying dead at this very moment.

Cosnet came back with the ropes.

"Ben's gone to find a cart to take them devils to the Police. I be thinking, my Lord, if they recovers from their wounds, they'll be deported."

"They will undoubtedly end up in prison for some years, so I don't think we need to worry about them."

"It's a good thing you was armed, my Lord."

Newman was passing through the door dragging the second and third men, while Cosnet had already pulled the first man into the passage.

Benina guessed that they would stay there until Ben brought a cart round to the front door.

David picked up the Russians' rifles and put them on a side table.

"I expect the Police will need these as evidence."

Then, as he turned round, he saw Benina looking at him, her blue eyes wide and frightened.

For a moment they just looked at each other and then with a little sob she cried,

"They would have killed you – "

As she spoke the tears ran down her cheeks.

David put his arms round her.

"But it was you who saved me, Benina, when you advised me to carry a revolver and you shot that man who would have killed me."

"I was terrified, so very terrified."

She looked up at him as she spoke.

Then David's lips were on hers.

At first he kissed Benina gently as if he would kiss away her tears.

Then as he could feel the softness and innocence of her lips, his arms tightened.

His kisses became more demanding.

He knew as he had realised already that she loved him.

It was a different love from anything he had ever known in his life.

A love, which, although he had not really admitted it, he had sought, but thought he would never find.

He kissed her until they were both breathless.

Then he suggested gently,

"You must go to bed, my darling, I must see first to these men being taken away, then we can both rest without worrying."

"Thank God, you are safe," murmured Benina.

"Absolutely safe and all thanks to you. So now my precious, do what I want you to do and in the morning we will talk about it all again."

As he spoke and was about to take his arms from her, he suddenly felt something strike him on his forehead.

It made him start.

And then as he looked to see what it could be, he was struck again.

Benina gave a cry.

"*Look*, look!" she cried and pointed to the ceiling.

David looked up.

As he did so another coin would have struck him if he had not stepped to one side.

As he had fallen, the bullet from the first Russian's rifle had made a hole in the ceiling and now it was easy to see the plaster of the ceiling was falling gradually away.

As it did so more gold coins fell with a crash onto the floor.

Both David and Benina were speechless.

Then she called out,

"*It's the treasure*! We have found it! We have just found it, David!"

Her voice broke and once again tears were running down her cheeks.

David put his arms around her.

"We have found it, my darling, and now everything will be exactly as we want it to be."

Then he was kissing her again.

Kissing her for sheer joy.

When their lips were not held by each other's, they were laughing.

At the eleventh hour everything was wonderful!

It was a long time later before he could persuade Benina that they must go upstairs.

By this time a large number of gold coins had fallen into a pile on the carpet.

She kept turning them over in her hands as if even now she could not believe they were real.

When they eventually left, the passage was empty and the front door closed. Newman and Cosnet must have driven their prisoners away in triumph.

They walked together upstairs and David said,

"I think that neither of us will sleep if we do not see exactly how my grandfather hid his treasure in the floor. I must admit it never occurred to me."

"The floors are so strongly built. I cannot imagine how he managed it."

They went into the Master bedroom.

With a cleverness no one would have credited him

with, the Marquis had succeeded in dislodging one of the heavy beams directly under his bed.

He had sawn through one of the strong beams used by the Elizabethan builders.

Between the floor of the Master bedroom and the ceiling of the study there was a whole foot of empty space and that was where he had deposited his precious money.

Then he refitted the beam back so exactly that the Marquis would know that no one would look for it there unless they had taken the whole house to pieces.

David let Benina look and touch it and then he put the beam back into its place.

"We are both tired, and quite frankly I need help to move that lot, exhausting though it may be!"

Benina laughed.

"You will undoubtedly sleep well on top of it and have very happy dreams."

"Very happy dreams," repeated David, "and you, my darling, will have them too."

"I love you, David. Do you *really* love me?"

He knew that she was thinking that perhaps he had kissed her only in the excitement of the moment.

"I have loved you for a long time, my Benina, but I would not admit it to myself because I had nothing to offer you – nothing except a large house and very little food."

"That is all over now!"

"It most certainly is. Now go to bed, my beautiful darling, because I have lots of plans for tomorrow."

"I want to help you with all of them."

"They could not be carried out without you."

He put his arms round her and drew her out of his room and along to her own.

When they were inside her bedroom, he lifted her up and placed her gently on the bed.

"You have been more wonderful, my Benina, than I can possibly tell you, but we will discuss it all tomorrow."

He kissed her very tenderly and very lovingly.

Before she could protest, he left the room, closing the door behind him.

For a moment she could hardly believe that he had gone.

Then she began to realise what had happened.

What was more important than finding the treasure was that David loved her.

And then she began to pray.

'Thank you, dear God, for your love and his,' she prayed over and over again until she fell asleep.

*

It was Nanny who woke Benina the next morning.

She came bustling in and pulled back the curtains.

"I've never heard such a to-do and to think I slept all though it and missed the fun. It's more than I can bear."

"Oh, Nanny it is *so* so wonderful!"

"It certainly is. You've got to hurry now, 'cos his Lordship wants to be off to Canterbury the moment you've finished breakfast."

Benina laughed.

"Of course he wants to take the money back to the Bank. We cannot risk it staying here when anyone might help themselves to it."

"If you asks me they'd have to be clairvoyant to do so. When I sees the place where the old Lord has hid it, I have to say it were very clever of him."

"Very clever indeed."

Nanny helped her into the best of her dresses.

It was not particularly smart, but at least Nanny had mended it by covering up some of the worst patches with little bows of ribbon.

Benina's hat was pretty as it had been trimmed to match her dress and she carried it in her hand as she went downstairs.

She had already learnt that David had been up since six and he and Newman had retrieved all the money from its hiding place and packed it into trunks.

Benina, however, was not thinking of the money as she walked into the dining room.

She was thinking just how much she loved David and praying that he would still love her as he had said he did last night.

When their eyes met, she knew she had no need to be anxious.

Because they were alone, she ran towards him.

He put his arms round her and held her against him, but he did not kiss her.

"We have so much to do today, and if I start kissing you now, my sweetness, you will never have breakfast and we shall be standing here until it is dark."

Benina laughed.

"I never thought I would sleep last night, but I did, and when Nanny called me, I thought for a moment it was all a dream."

"It was a bad dream and a nightmare we will never experience again."

Newman came in with Benina's breakfast and she realised that David had already eaten.

"We are going to Canterbury today," he said, "and everyone is coming with us. Just in case by some ghastly chance we are held up and robbed on the way, we will all be armed!"

"I cannot imagine it, but do not let us take any risks after all that has happened – "

"I have no intention of doing so, and that is why I am taking everyone with me and they will be told exactly what they have to do when we reach Canterbury."

He thought as he spoke how surprised Mr. Morley would be when after all they appeared with the two million pounds.

Because she realised he was in such a hurry, Benina ate her breakfast quickly.

Even so, when she put on her hat and picked up her bag that concealed her revolver, David was already in the carriage outside.

Nanny was just joining him and as she came down the steps, Newman closed the front door and locked it.

Benina saw that Ben was driving and his father sat beside him.

Newman and Nanny were inside the carriage with their backs to the horse whilst she and David sat opposite them in the best seats.

The two trunks of money were on the floor between them and they would have made it rather uncomfortable if they had not rested their legs on top of them.

Benina slipped her hand into David's hoping that Nanny and Newman would not notice.

"This is so exciting," she cried.

"I thought you would think so and now that we are on our way to Canterbury, I will tell you exactly what we are going to do when we arrive."

"I've been waiting to hear that," said Nanny, "and it's so kind of your Lordship to include me in the party and I'm not pretending it's not a great experience for me."

"If it had not been for you, Nanny, we would not have got through all the work," David told her. "And in future you will be able to put your feet up, as they are now, and give your orders to cooks, scullions and at least half-a-dozen housemaids!"

Nanny giggled.

"I'll believe that when I sees them!"

"You *will* see them. Newman is coming with me to the agency to see how many experienced staff we can find for the senior jobs, while all the less demanding ones will be filled by people from the village.

"Now what you have to do, Nanny, is to take Miss Benina to best shop in Canterbury – I am sure there will be someone to tell you where it is – and buy her a wedding dress."

"*A wedding dress!*" exclaimed Nanny.

Benina glanced at David and he thought no woman could look more radiant or more beautiful.

"I have already sent a letter to the Vicar to ask him to marry us tonight at six o'clock."

He turned to look at Benina as he spoke and then he breathed very softly,

"Will that suit you, my precious Benina?"

She could only just whisper the word 'yes' and he realised that there was no need for words.

With an effort he spoke to Nanny.

"Benina will want every sort of clothes available, and as soon as we go to London, I will buy her a trousseau which will be better and smarter than any other girl in the *Beau Monde* has ever possessed!"

"That's something I wants to hear, and you can be quite sure, my Lord, we'll not disappoint you."

"You will have quite a lot of time to buy what you require, because I am going to call on the Archbishop of Canterbury to obtain a Special Licence."

"I'm sure there won't be any difficulty, my Lord," came in Newman.

"Lastly, Cosnet is to buy flowers for the Chapel. It may not be as clean as we would like, but he promises to do his best and we do not want anyone else to know what occurred last night until the money is safely in the hands of the Bank Manager."

"That is so sensible of you," said Benina. "As you say, David, it would be dreadful if anyone held us up and prevented us reaching the Bank."

She need not have worried as everything went just as David had planned.

It was only as the men carried the trunks into the Bank Manager's private room that he thought Mr. Morley would have a stroke when he saw what they contained.

"I can scarcely believe my eyes, my Lord. It seems impossible that so much money, which has been hidden for so long, has come back to us."

"Now it is back in your keeping and I want most of it invested immediately in really safe shares that will pay good dividends now and in the future."

"You can leave it to us, my Lord, and I promise that you will not be disappointed."

Mr. Morley kept glancing down at the money as if he could not really believe it was there.

David left him and went off to see the Archbishop, who asked him to go to his private apartment.

The Archbishop of Canterbury greeted David with outstretched hands.

"It is delightful to meet you, my Lord. I heard you were home, but was told that things were very difficult for you which I must say I rather expected."

"Very difficult indeed, Your Grace."

Because he thought it only right for the Archbishop to know everything, he told him the whole story, while at the same time suggesting it would be a great mistake if it was known to everyone.

"I will of course tell the world that your grandfather was merely neglectful of the estate in his old age and did not realise what poverty and depression he was causing."

"It will all be put right now, Your Grace, and of course I will see to the Church, which also requires repair like everything else in the house and in the village."

"I should be most grateful if you could, and I am sure you will realise that the stipend the Vicar has received has been very small. Although I did try to speak to your grandfather, he would not listen to me."

"I will put it right," promised David, "and I would like to give a donation of thankfulness to go to any charity in the County you think is in need of it."

The Archbishop thanked him again and blessed him before he left.

When he had returned to the carriage, they drove to where they had agreed to pick up Nanny and Benina.

It was rather a long wait.

When they came there was a large number of shop assistants carrying dress boxes and hatboxes and somehow they managed to pile everything into the carriage.

Once again they had to travel with their legs resting on boxes between the seats and on top were a great number of flowers that Cosnet had bought.

It was almost impossible for them to see Nanny and

Newman on the other side and it was difficult for David to hold Benina's hand, but only to kiss it.

He felt a little quiver course through him as he did so and knew that the same was happening to her.

Newman had bought a case of fine champagne and placed an order for several more cases of wine to follow as well as a wedding cake, although for the moment it was to be kept a secret from Benina.

So that she should not see it, it was up on the front of the carriage and held in place by Cosnet.

When they returned to Ingle Hall, there was no time for Benina to talk to David as she so wanted to do.

Nanny insisted she should have a bath and Cosnet carried up the hot and cold water to her bedroom.

The wedding dress was simply lovely – it had been expensive and was actually a show-gown to be put in the window to attract other brides to the shop.

After she had finished her bath Nanny dressed her, making her hair look really glorious and as she was putting in the final touches, Newman came in with the family tiara as well as a veil that he had found in a box in the safe.

There was an old diamond necklace to match the tiara and two diamond bracelets to wear on her wrists.

When she looked in the mirror, Benina could hardly believe she was still herself.

She was sure as she went downstairs that her father and mother would be proud of her.

David was waiting for her in the study dressed in his smartest uniform.

For one moment they just looked at each other.

Then he offered her his arm.

Slowly they walked down the long corridor that led to the one at the end of which was the Chapel.

As they did so Benina was aware that Nanny had slipped down from another staircase and would already be waiting for them.

Only the people who had been part of their life in these last desperate days of hunting for the money were to be the witnesses at their wedding.

When they reached the door of the Chapel, Benina gave a gasp.

Cosnet had certainly made the Chapel look so very different from when she had last seen it.

There seemed to be flowers everywhere and three candles were alight on the altar.

The Vicar was waiting for them wearing a white embroidered surplice.

It was a simple Service and the Vicar read it with a sincerity that was deeply moving.

When they finally knelt at the altar to receive the blessing, Benina was certain her father and mother were looking down, thrilled and delighted that she had found the same love they had known and which was still with them in Heaven.

She was sure that it was their help and her prayers that had saved David's life and made it possible for her to be his wife.

'*I love him*, I love him,' she wanted to shout out.

But the words vibrated in her heart and she felt that they were repeated by songs of angels as David drew her to her feet.

He pulled back her veil and kissed her very gently.

She knew that it was not only a kiss of dedication and Holiness, but also one of such perfect happiness that it could not be expressed in any other way.

When the ceremony was over they all went into the

library where Newman offered them glasses of champagne and pieces of wedding cake.

Benina cut the cake, as was correct, with a sword that David had used when he was a soldier in India.

She sent up a fervent prayer as she did so that he would never have need to use a sword or his revolver again against an enemy.

Then they were all drinking the health of the bride and bridegroom and the room was filled with laughter.

*

Later David and Benina dined alone and enjoyed a delicious dinner cooked naturally by Nanny.

Afterwards it was impossible for them to remember what they had eaten – they had only known that they were together.

When they gazed into each other's eyes, they forgot what they were saying.

When dinner was over, they went back to the study for a last look at the wedding cake and more important to look up at the ceiling.

There was a large empty hole above them.

"We ought to put a plaque on it," laughed Benina.

"We will never forget how we found it, because never again, my dearest darling, do I want you to come into contact with anything so unpleasant or ugly as an avenging Russian."

Benina put out her hand to him.

"You don't think they will try again?"

David shook his head.

"No. One thing I will say in their favour is that, if they fail in a project, they invariably, so we found in India, concentrate on their next objective."

Benina put her arms around him.

"I suppose I shall always be frightened of losing you, David."

"You will never lose me, Benina, as we are part of each other for ever – and now, my precious, beautiful and glorious wife, I am going to teach you about love."

He kissed her tenderly.

"I think it is a subject you know very little about."

It was later that evening when they were together in the Master bedroom and David was kissing her until she felt as if the stars themselves had fallen down from the sky.

"I love you, I adore you," he kept saying.

Benina found it impossible to say anything, only to feel the wonder of his kisses and the touch of his hands.

It was so exhilarating and there were no words she could find to express the wonder of her sensations.

It was then she mumbled almost in a whisper,

"You said you would teach me about love, darling David. Please, you must teach me to love you as you want to be loved. I am so afraid of disappointing you."

"You could never disappoint me, Benina, you are everything I believe a woman should be, but at the same time I did not think anyone so perfect and so wonderful could possibly exist in this world."

"I will try to be everything you want me to be, and it is so marvellous being with you that I feel we are already in Heaven."

"That is exactly what we will go on feeling and, my precious, we will make this house so beautiful and so filled with our love that everyone who comes here will feel that we have bequeathed them some of our happiness."

"Only you could think of that, David, and of course it is just what I want to happen too."

"Miracles have happened already and miracles will happen again in the future. It is you, my darling, who will make the miracles true and real, not only for me but for all those who crave to be as happy as we are."

Benina put her arms round his neck.

"I love you and my love is so overwhelming that I am frightened I will wake up and find it is only a dream."

"It *is* a dream, Benina, but we are going to live it not only for this life but for all Eternity and perhaps even longer."

Then he was kissing her.

Kissing her until they both felt that they were flying into the sky and as he made her his they touched the Divine Love which is God and which would be theirs forever.